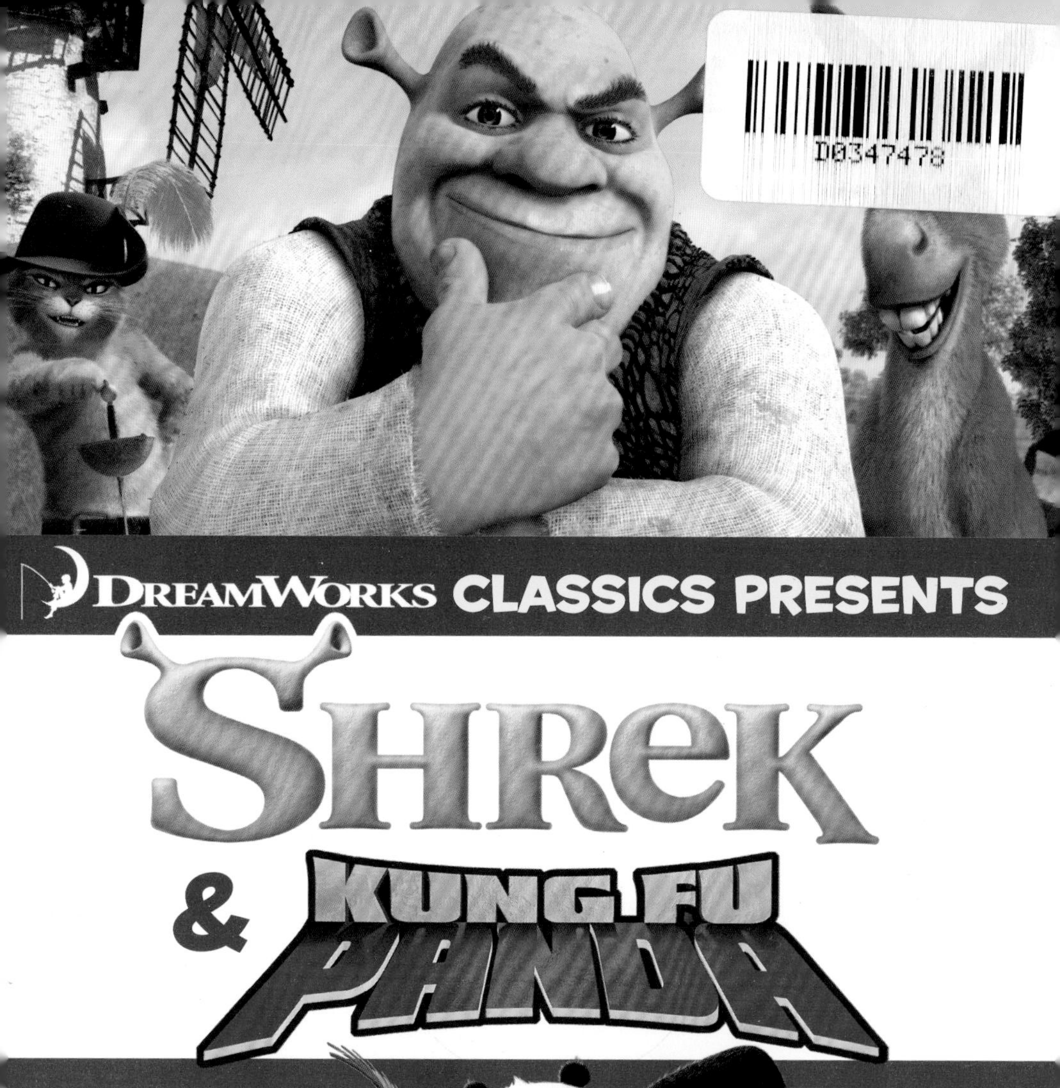

DREAMWORKS CLASSICS PRESENTS

SHREK & KUNG FU PANDA

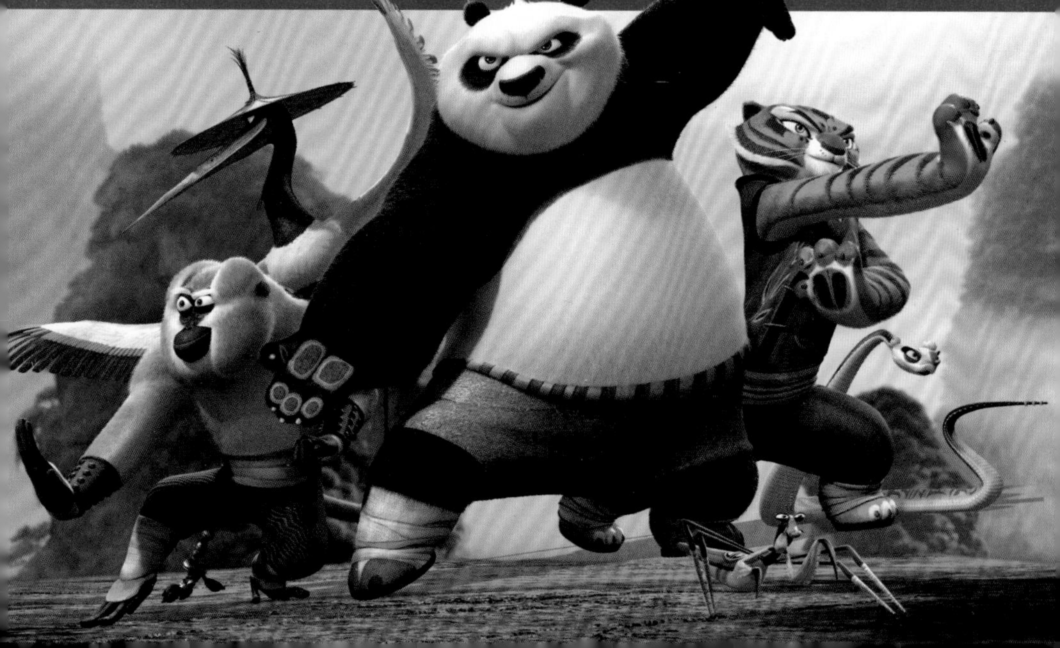

CONTENTS

KUNG FU PANDA COMICS!

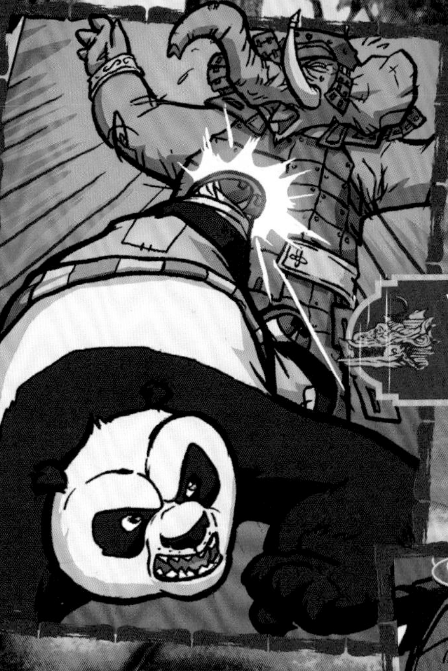

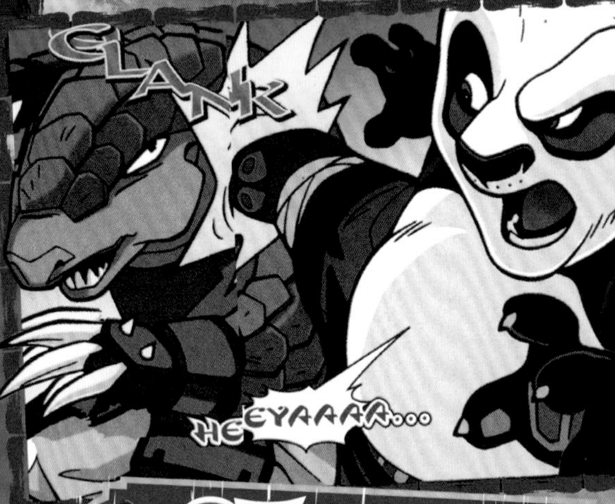

CLANK
HEEYAAAA...

TITAN COMICS
SENIOR EDITOR Martin Eden
PRODUCTION MANAGER Obi Onuora
PRODUCTION SUPERVISORS Maria James, Jackie Flook
PRODUCTION ASSISTANT Peter James
STUDIO MANAGER Selina Juneja
SENIOR SALES MANAGER Steve Tothill
MARKETING MANAGER Ricky Claydon
PUBLISHING MANAGER Darryl Tothill
PUBLISHING DIRECTOR Chris Teather
OPERATIONS DIRECTOR Leigh Baulch
EXECUTIVE DIRECTOR Vivian Cheung
PUBLISHER Nick Landau

ISBN: 9781782762478

Published by Titan Comics, a division of Titan Publishing Group Ltd. 144 Southwark St. London, SE1 0UP.

10 9 8 7 6 5 4 3 2 1

First printed in China in December 2015. A CIP catalogue record for this title is available from the British Library. Titan Comics. TC0553

Special thanks to Andrew James, Steve White and Donna Askem.

DreamWorks CLASSICS PRESENTS

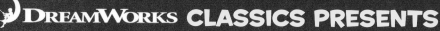

Shrek & Kung Fu Panda

SHREK STORIES!

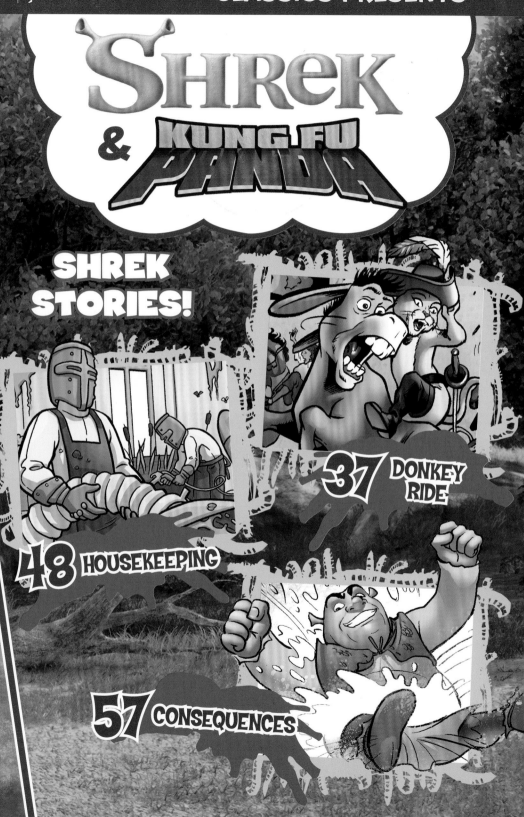

KUNG FU PANDA

PO

Po's an apprentice noodle maker with a massive interest in the arts – and stars – of kung fu. In his dreams, he's the fastest, most powerful martial arts master alive, beloved across the whole of China. In reality, he's swiftly following his father into the family business, with nothing special on the horizon bar finally discovering the secret family recipe. But a trip to watch the next Dragon Warrior being chosen soon turns into a date with destiny – and for Po, nothing will ever be the same again!

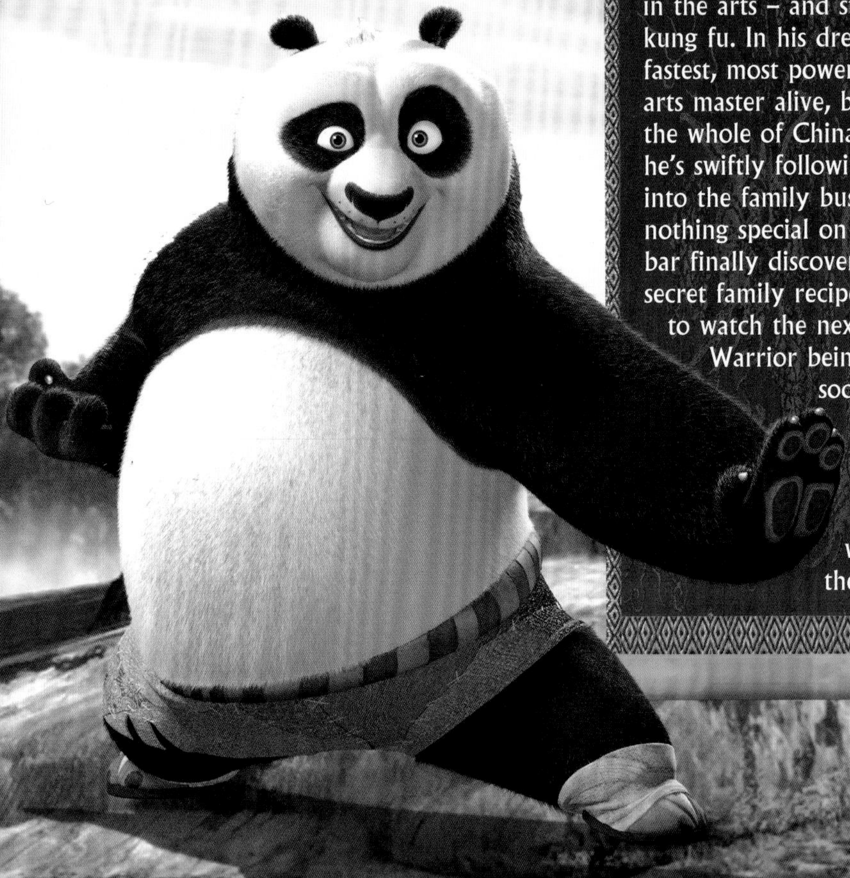

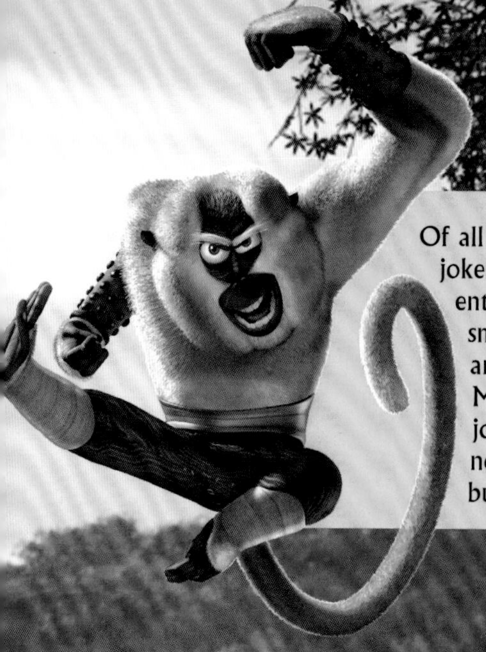

MONKEY

Of all the martial arts masters, Monkey is the joker of the bunch. Mischievous, playful, and enthusiastic, Master Monkey is more street-smart than the rest of the Furious Five and an unpredictable prankser. Don't think Monkey's laidback attitude, his practical jokes and his 'fun' personality mean he's not serious about kung fu. Monkey means business when it comes to kicking butt!

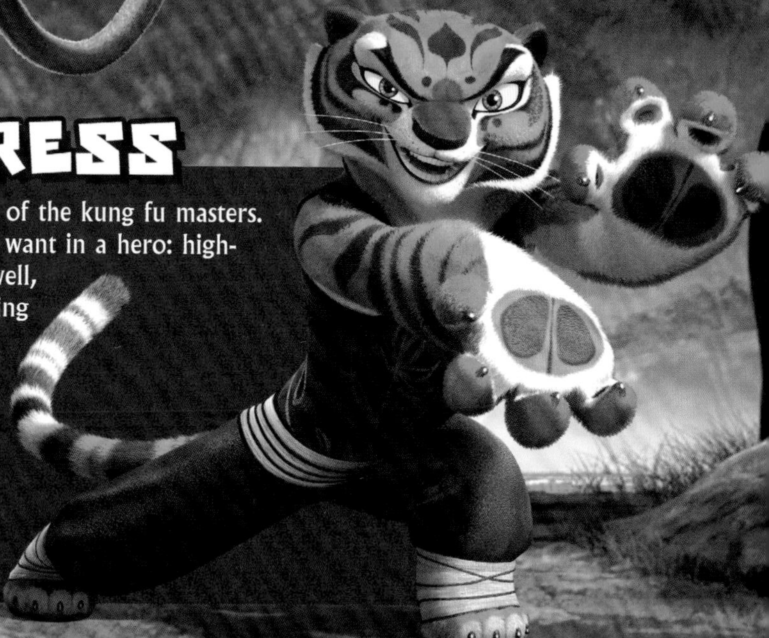

TIGRESS

Tigress is the strongest of the kung fu masters. She's everything you'd want in a hero: high-achieving, brave and, well, heroic! She'd do anything to save the day. She's unwaveringly loyal to Po and what he represents as the Dragon Warrior. But underneath her stoic exterior is sincere compassion.

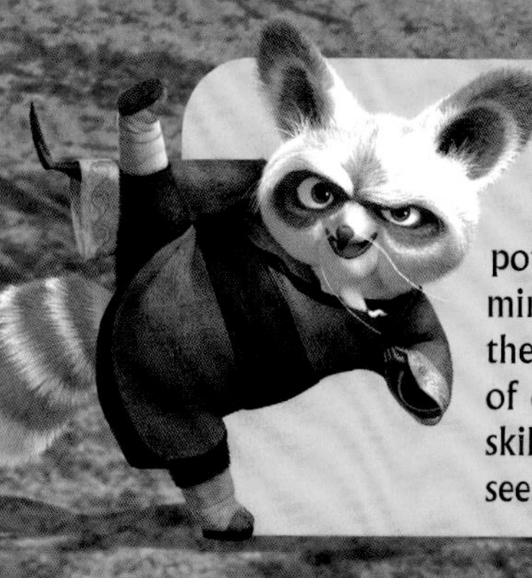

SHIFU

Master Shifu is the trainer of the Furious Five. He's a strict, disciplined teacher who pushes his students to achieve their greatest potential. Shifu exerts maximum force with minimal effort, exemplified by his signature move, the Wuxi Finger Hold, with which he is capable of overpowering the strongest opponent. Shifu's skills border on the mystical--he often appears seemingly within the blink of an eye.

THE WARLORD OF SHADOW ISLAND

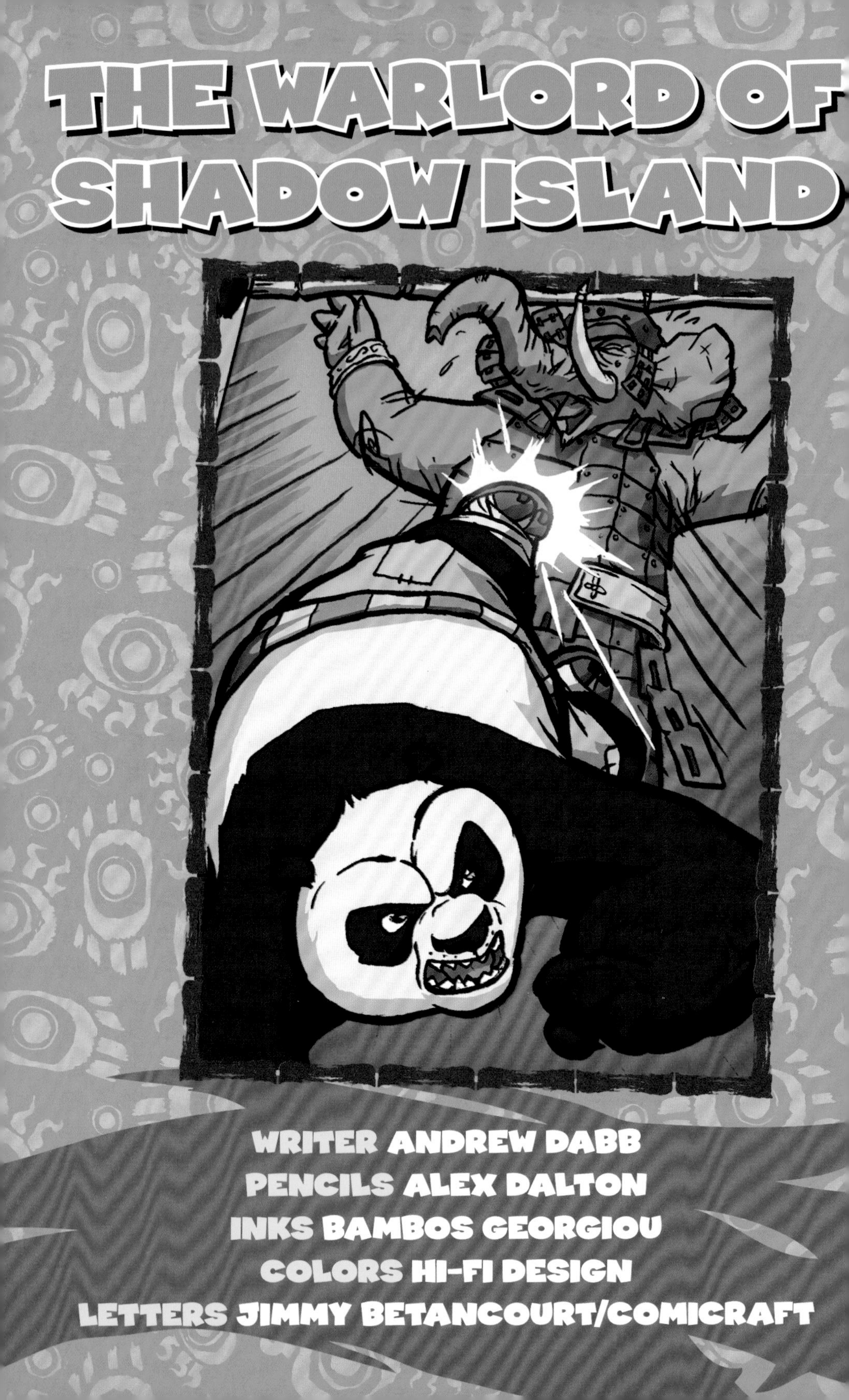

WRITER ANDREW DABB
PENCILS ALEX DALTON
INKS BAMBOS GEORGIOU
COLORS HI-FI DESIGN
LETTERS JIMMY BETANCOURT/COMICRAFT

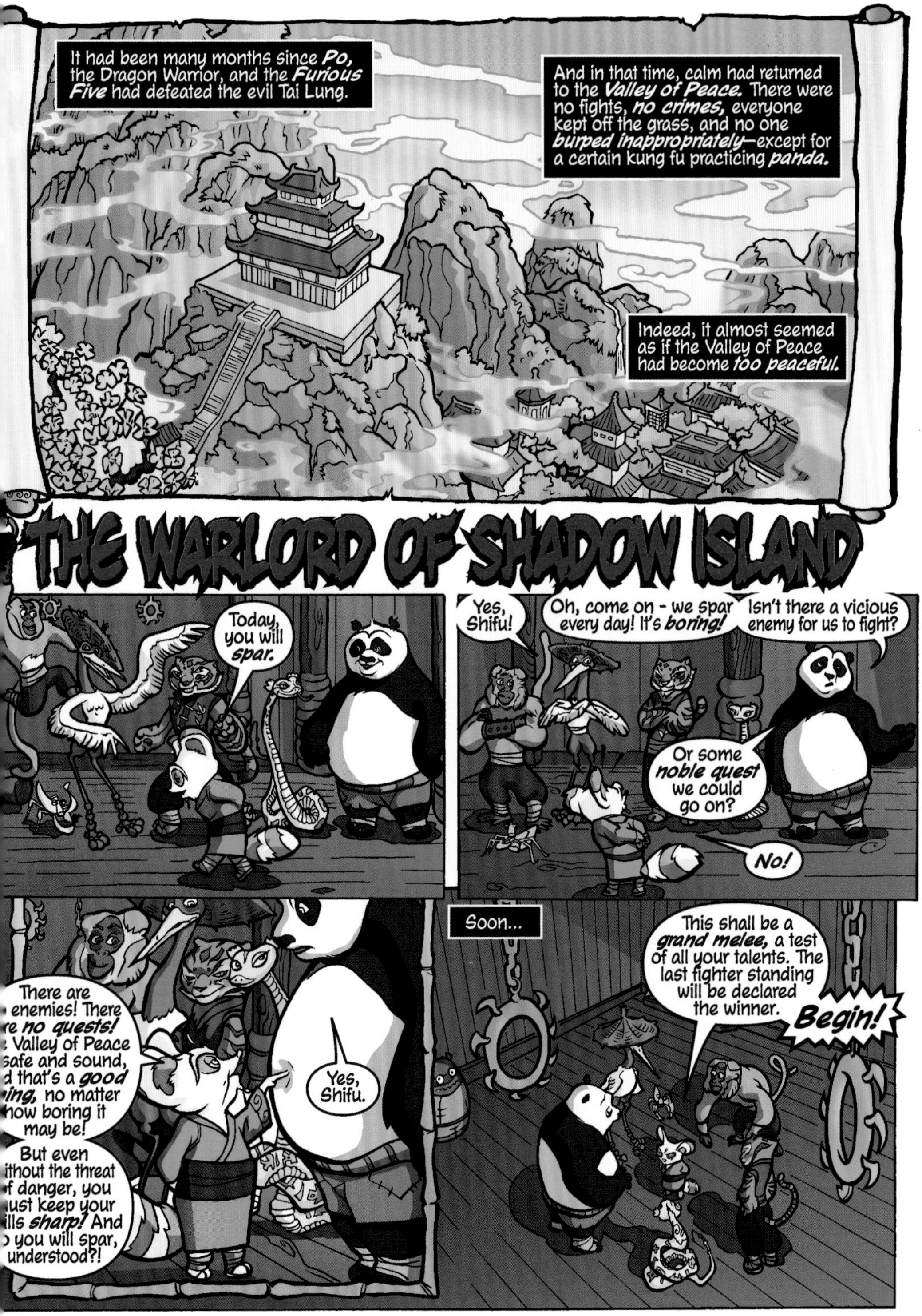

It had been many months since Po, the Dragon Warrior, and the Furious Five had defeated the evil Tai Lung.
And in that time, calm had returned to the Valley of Peace. There were no fights, no crimes, everyone kept off the grass, and no one burped inappropriately—except for a certain kung fu practicing panda.
Indeed, it almost seemed as if the Valley of Peace had become too peaceful.
THE WARLORD OF SHADOW ISLAND
Today, you will spar.
Yes, Shifu!
Oh, come on - we spar every day! It's boring!
Isn't there a vicious enemy for us to fight?
Or some noble quest we could go on?
No!
There are enemies! There re no quests! Valley of Peace safe and sound, d that's a good ing, no matter how boring it may be!
But even ithout the threat f danger, you ust keep your ills sharp! And you will spar, understood?!
Yes, Shifu.
Soon...
This shall be a grand melee, a test of all your talents. The last fighter standing will be declared the winner.
Begin!

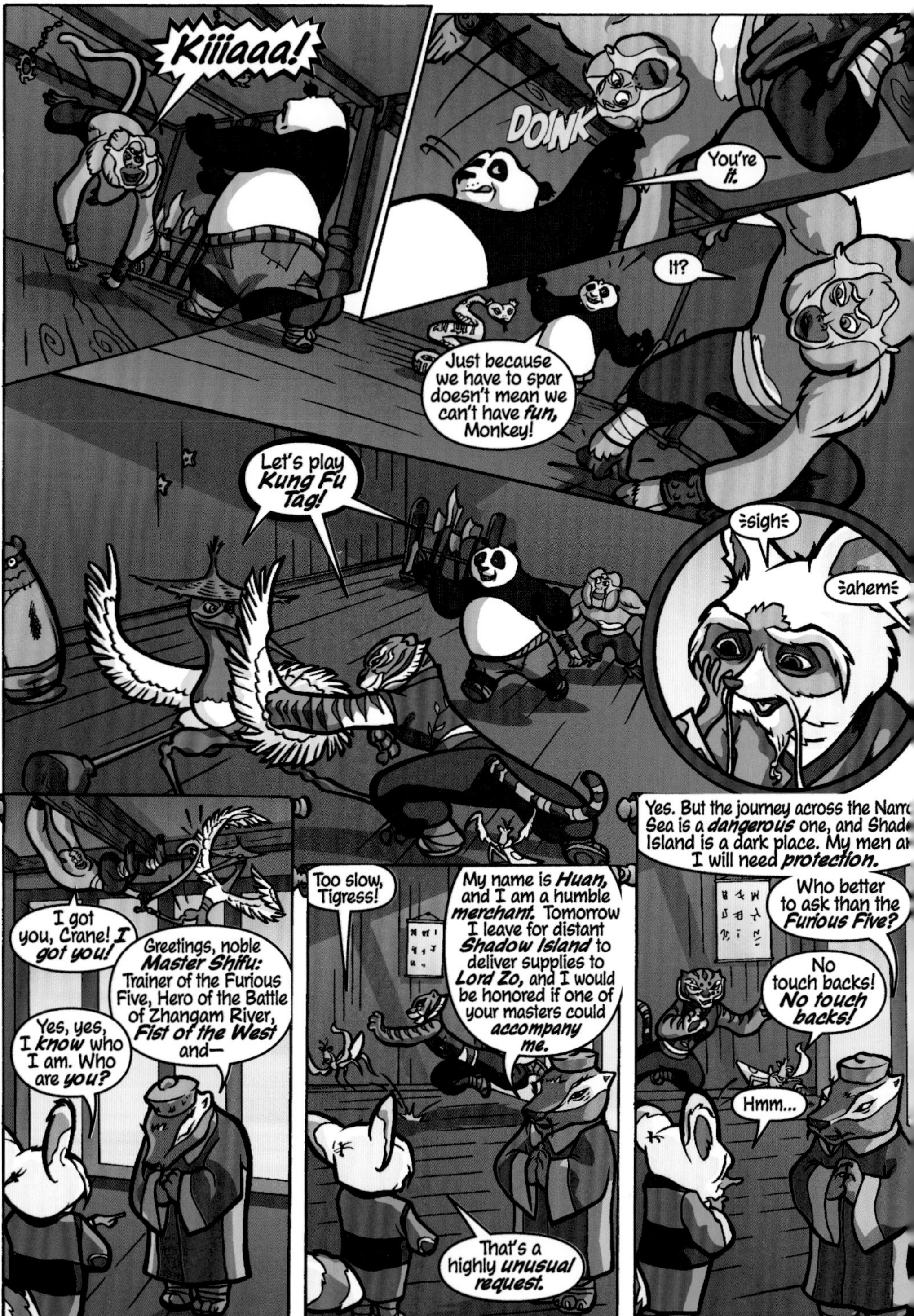
Kiiiaaa!
DOINK
You're it.
It?
Just because we have to spar doesn't mean we can't have fun, Monkey!
Let's play Kung Fu Tag!
sigh
ahem
I got you, Crane! I got you!
Greetings, noble Master Shifu: Trainer of the Furious Five, Hero of the Battle of Zhangam River, Fist of the West and—
Yes, yes, I know who I am. Who are you?
Too slow, Tigress!
My name is Huan, and I am a humble merchant. Tomorrow I leave for distant Shadow Island to deliver supplies to Lord Zo, and I would be honored if one of your masters could accompany me.
That's a highly unusual request.
Who better to ask than the Furious Five?
No touch backs! No touch backs!
Hmm...

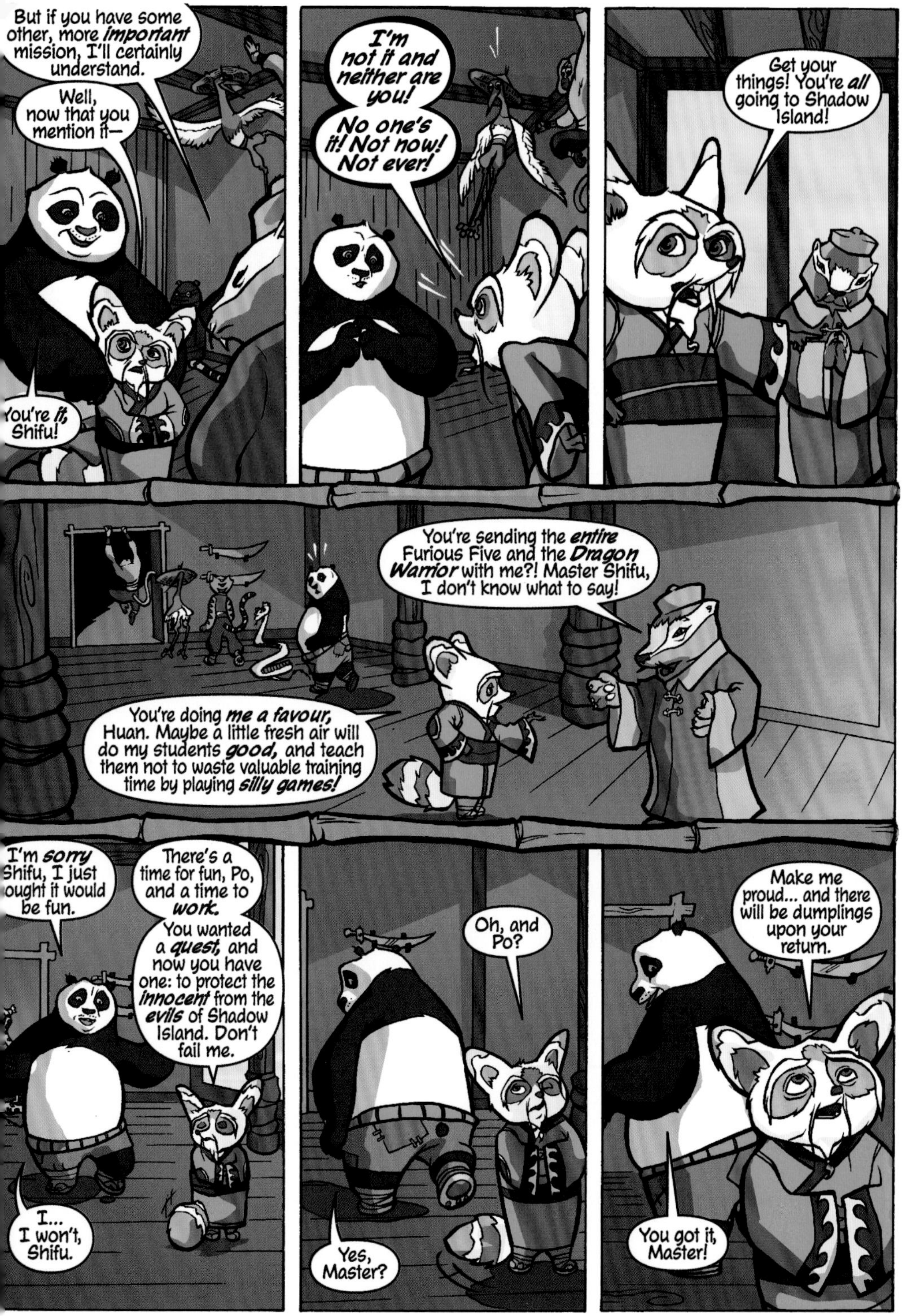

But if you have some other, more important mission, I'll certainly understand.
Well, now that you mention it—
You're it, Shifu!
I'm not it and neither are you!
No one's it! Not now! Not ever!
Get your things! You're all going to Shadow Island!
You're sending the entire Furious Five and the Dragon Warrior with me?! Master Shifu, I don't know what to say!
You're doing me a favour, Huan. Maybe a little fresh air will do my students good, and teach them not to waste valuable training time by playing silly games!
I'm sorry Shifu, I just ought it would be fun.
There's a time for fun, Po, and a time to work.
You wanted a quest, and now you have one: to protect the innocent from the evils of Shadow Island. Don't fail me.
I... I won't, Shifu.
Oh, and Po?
Yes, Master?
Make me proud... and there will be dumplings upon your return.
You got it, Master!

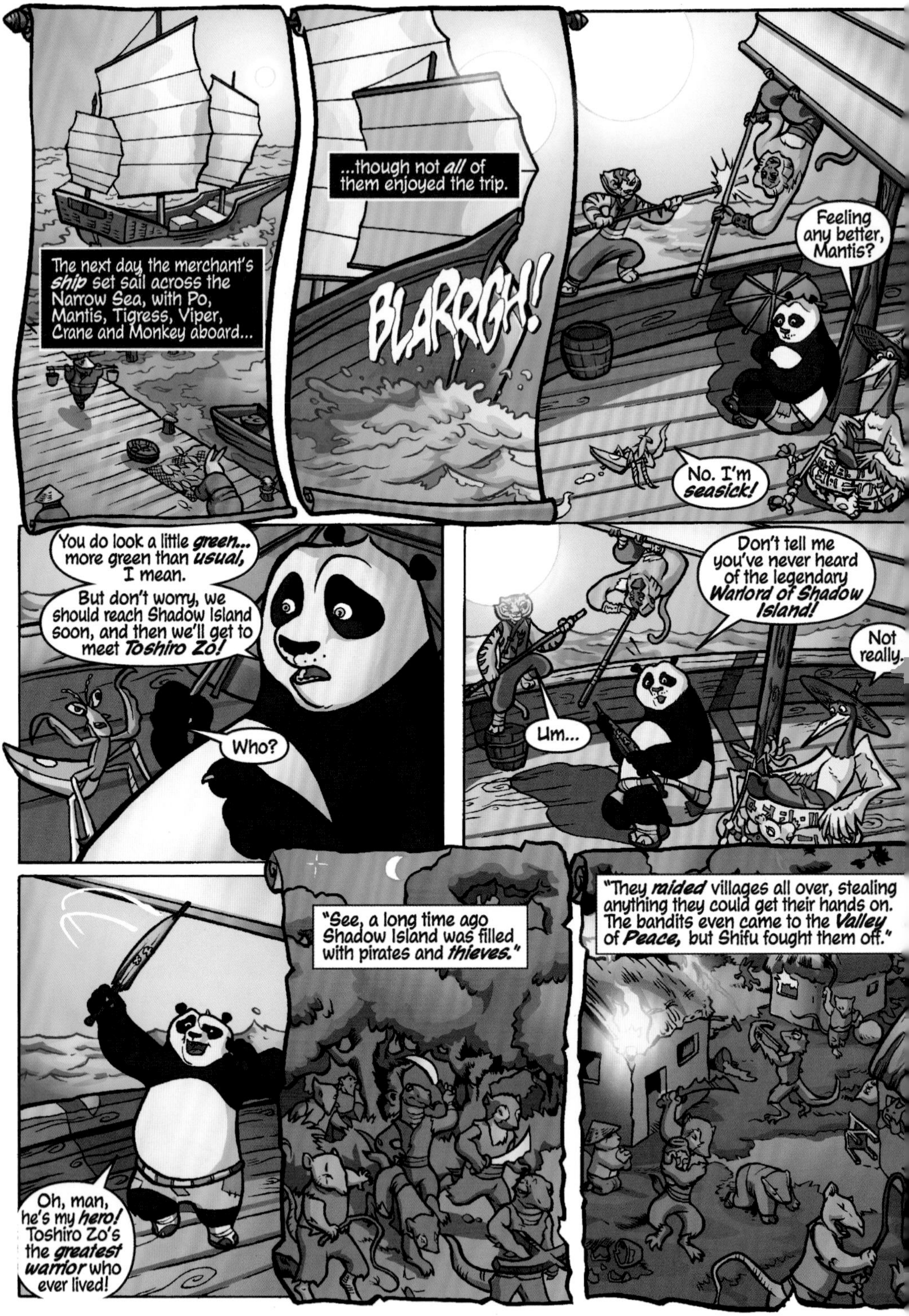
The next day the merchant's ship set sail across the Narrow Sea, with Po, Mantis, Tigress, Viper, Crane and Monkey aboard...
...though not all of them enjoyed the trip.
BLARRGH!
Feeling any better, Mantis?
No. I'm seasick!
You do look a little green... more green than usual, I mean.
But don't worry, we should reach Shadow Island soon, and then we'll get to meet Toshiro Zo!
Who?
Don't tell me you've never heard of the legendary Warlord of Shadow Island!
Not really.
Um...
Oh, man, he's my hero! Toshiro Zo's the greatest warrior who ever lived!
"See, a long time ago Shadow Island was filled with pirates and thieves."
"They raided villages all over, stealing anything they could get their hands on. The bandits even came to the Valley of Peace, but Shifu fought them off."

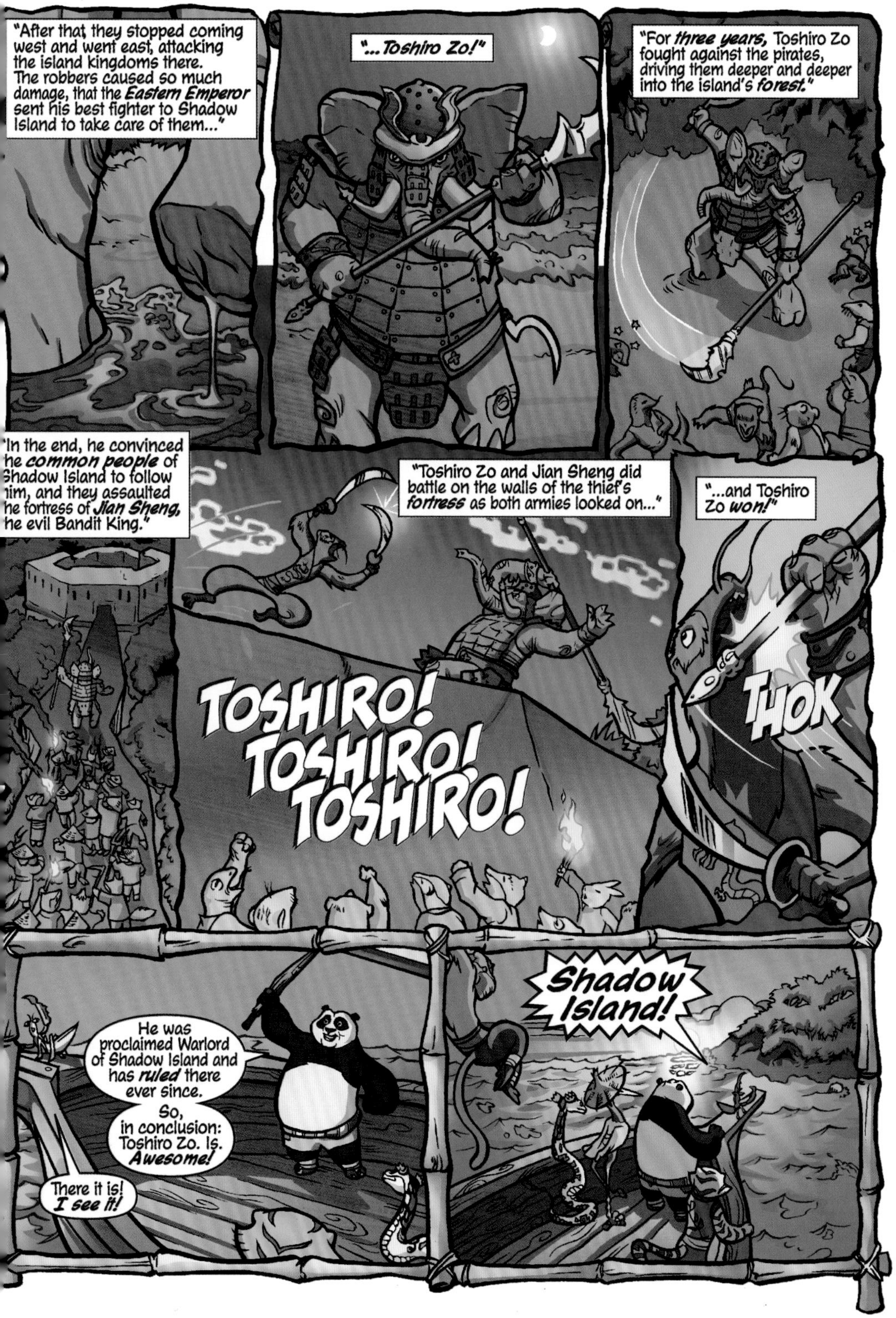
"After that, they stopped coming west and went east, attacking the island kingdoms there. The robbers caused so much damage, that the Eastern Emperor sent his best fighter to Shadow Island to take care of them..."
"...Toshiro Zo!"
"For three years, Toshiro Zo fought against the pirates, driving them deeper and deeper into the island's forest."
"In the end, he convinced the common people of Shadow Island to follow him, and they assaulted the fortress of Jian Sheng, the evil Bandit King."
"Toshiro Zo and Jian Sheng did battle on the walls of the thief's fortress as both armies looked on..."
TOSHIRO! TOSHIRO! TOSHIRO!
"...and Toshiro Zo won!"
THOK
He was proclaimed Warlord of Shadow Island and has ruled there ever since. So, in conclusion: Toshiro Zo. Is. Awesome!
There it is! I see it!
Shadow Island!

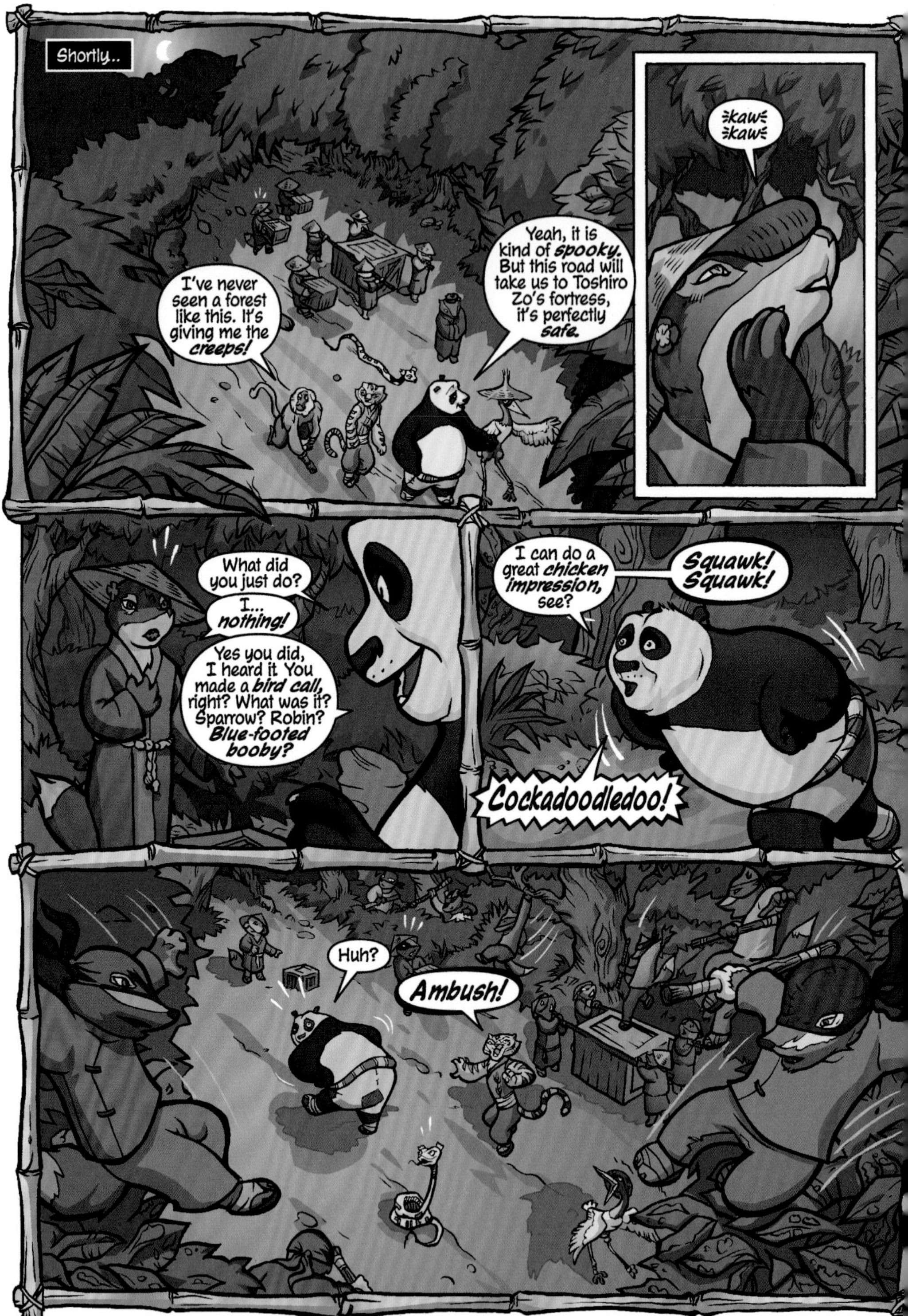
Shortly..
I've never seen a forest like this. It's giving me the creeps!
Yeah, it is kind of spooky. But this road will take us to Toshiro Zo's fortress, it's perfectly safe.
kaw kaw
What did you just do?
I... nothing!
Yes you did, I heard it You made a bird call, right? What was it? Sparrow? Robin? Blue-footed booby?
I can do a great chicken impression, see?
Squawk! Squawk!
Cockadoodledoo!
Huh?
Ambush!

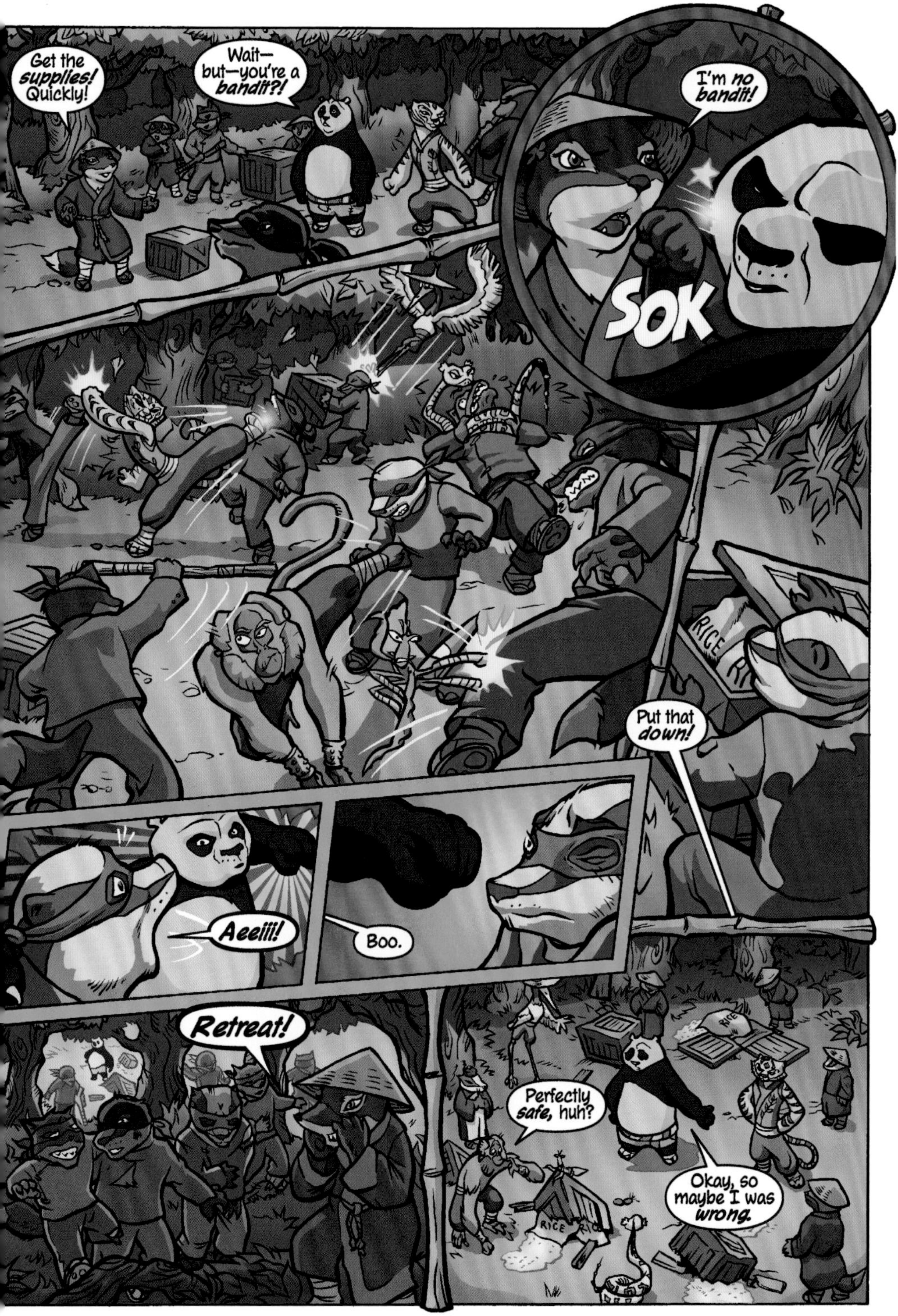
Get the supplies! Quickly!
Wait— but—you're a bandit?!
I'm no bandit!
SOK
Put that down!
Aeeiii!
Boo.
Retreat!
Perfectly safe, huh?
Okay, so maybe I was wrong.

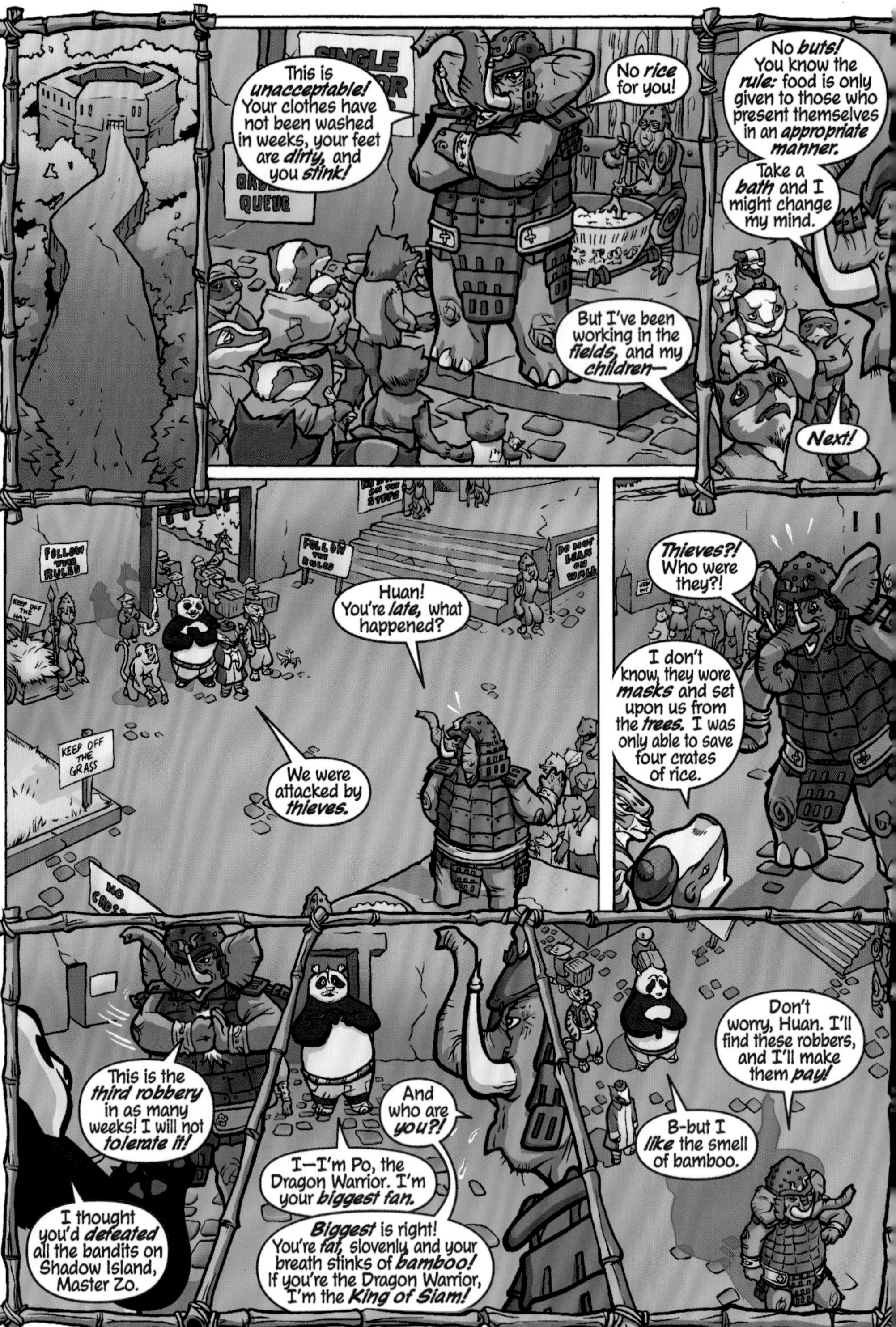

QUEUE
This is *unacceptable!* Your clothes have not been washed in weeks, your feet are *dirty,* and you *stink!*
No *rice* for you!
But I've been working in the *fields,* and my *children—*
No *buts!* You know the *rule:* food is only given to those who present themselves in an *appropriate manner.*
Take a *bath* and I might change my mind.
Next!
FOLLOW THE RULES
KEEP OFF THE HAY
FOLLOW THE RULES
DO NOT LEAN ON WALL
KEEP OFF THE GRASS
Huan! You're *late,* what happened?
We were attacked by *thieves.*
Thieves?! Who were they?!
I don't know, they wore *masks* and set upon us from the *trees.* I was only able to save four crates of rice.
This is the *third robbery* in as many weeks! I will not *tolerate it!*
I thought you'd *defeated* all the bandits on Shadow Island, Master Zo.
And who are *you?!*
I—I'm Po, the Dragon Warrior. I'm your *biggest fan.*
Biggest is right! You're *fat,* slovenly, and your breath stinks of *bamboo!* If you're the Dragon Warrior, I'm the *King of Siam!*
B-but I *like* the smell of bamboo.
Don't worry, Huan. I'll find these robbers, and I'll make them *pay!*

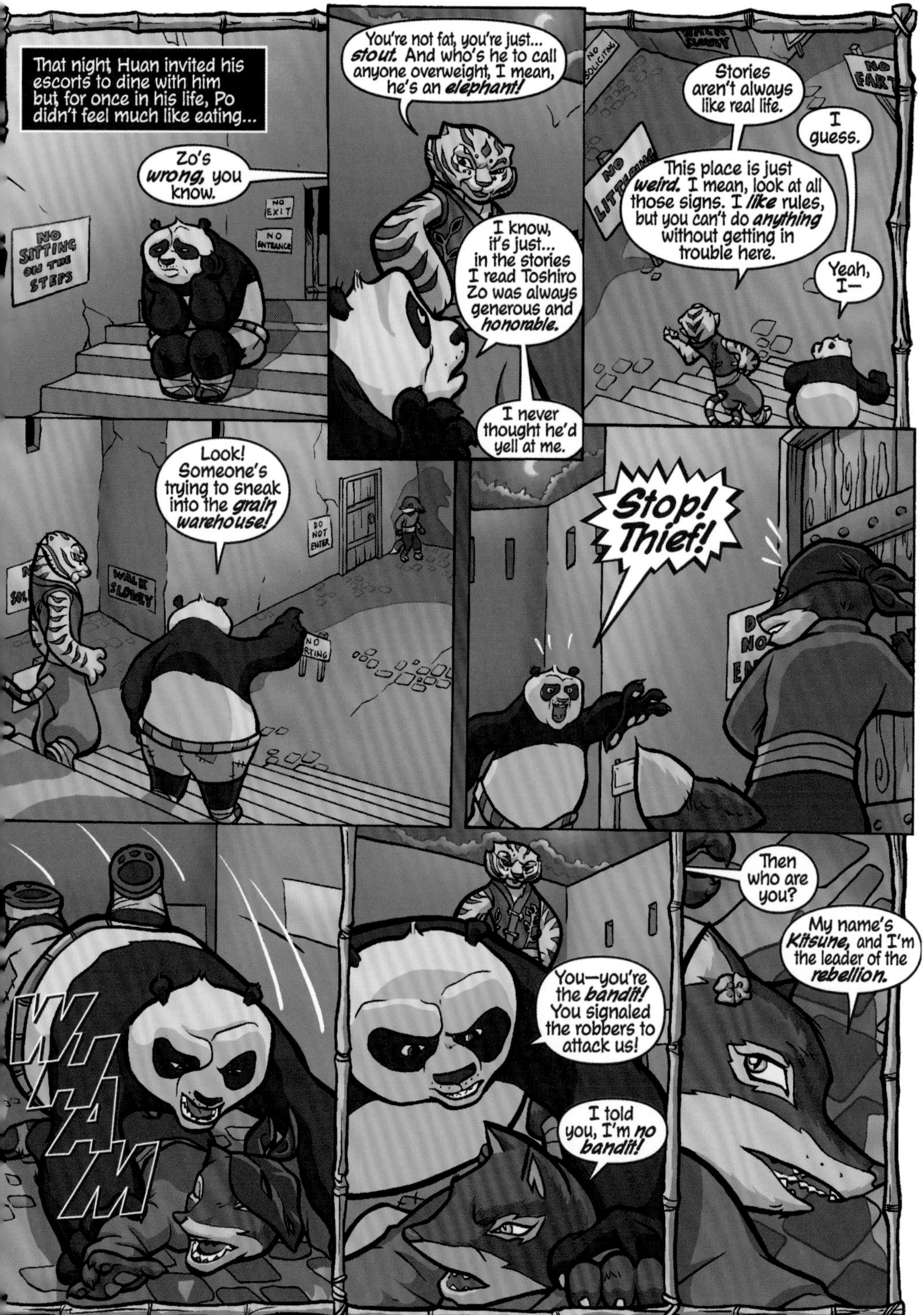

That night, Huan invited his escorts to dine with him but, for once in his life, Po didn't feel much like eating...
Zo's *wrong,* you know.
NO EXIT
NO ENTRANCE
NO SITTING ON THE STEPS
You're not fat, you're just... *stout.* And who's he to call anyone overweight, I mean, he's an *elephant!*
I know, it's just... in the stories I read Toshiro Zo was always generous and *honorable.*
I never thought he'd yell at me.
NO SOLICITING
Stories aren't always like real life.
I guess.
This place is just *weird.* I mean, look at all those signs. I *like* rules, but you can't do *anything* without getting in trouble here.
Yeah, I—
Look! Someone's trying to sneak into the *grain warehouse!*
WALK SLOWLY
DO NOT ENTER
Stop! Thief!
WHAM
Then who are you?
My name's *Kitsune,* and I'm the leader of the *rebellion.*
You—you're the *bandit!* You signaled the robbers to attack us!
I told you, I'm *no bandit!*

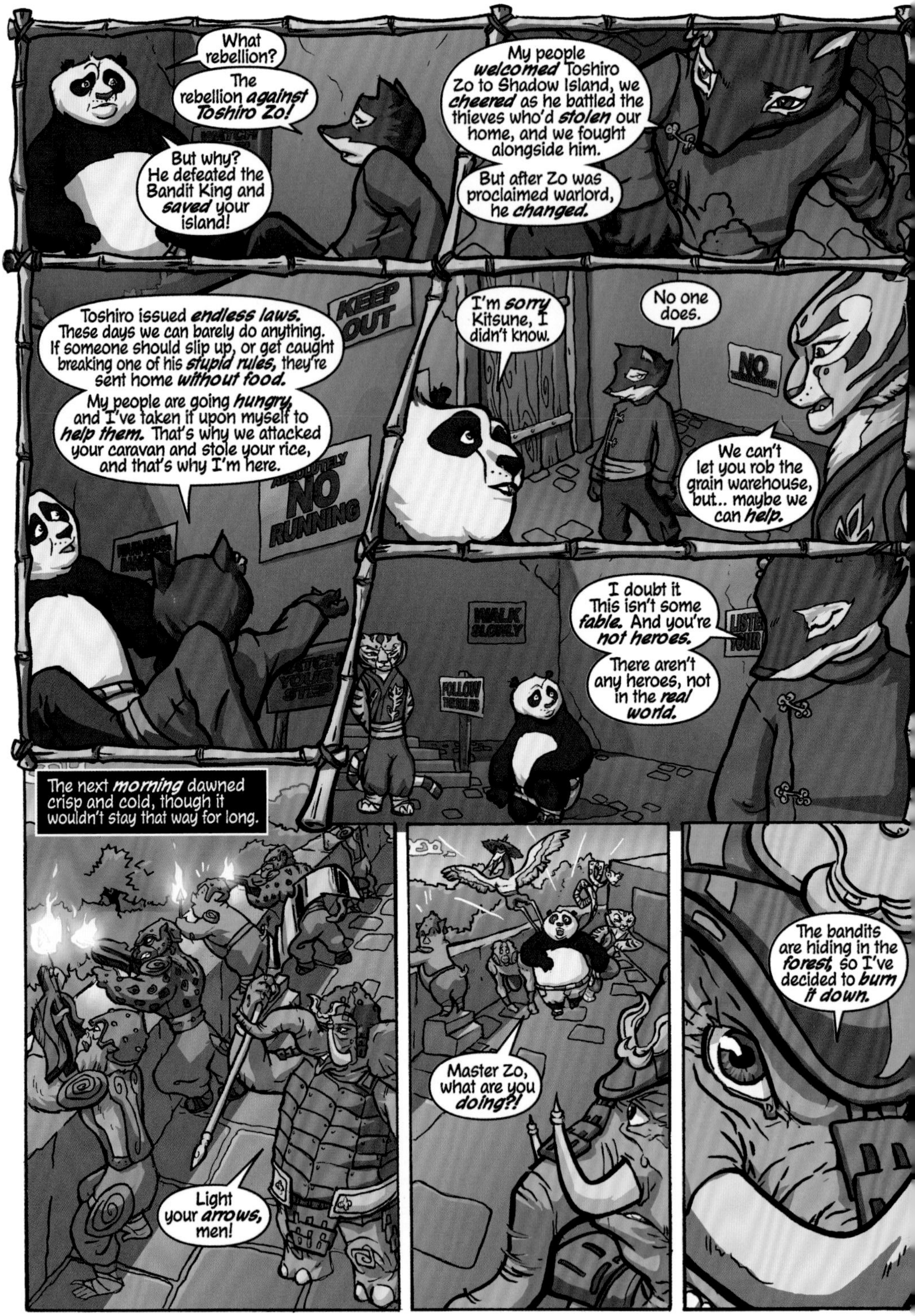

What rebellion?
The rebellion *against* *Toshiro Zo!*
But why? He defeated the Bandit King and *saved* your island!
My people *welcomed* Toshiro Zo to Shadow Island, we *cheered* as he battled the thieves who'd *stolen* our home, and we fought alongside him.
But after Zo was proclaimed warlord, he *changed.*
KEEP OUT
Toshiro issued *endless laws.* These days we can barely do anything. If someone should slip up, or get caught breaking one of his *stupid rules,* they're sent home *without food.*
My people are going *hungry,* and I've taken it upon myself to *help them.* That's why we attacked your caravan and stole your rice, and that's why I'm here.
ABSOLUTELY NO RUNNING
I'm *sorry* Kitsune, I didn't know.
No one does.
We can't let you rob the grain warehouse, but.. maybe we can *help.*
WALK SLOWLY
FOLLOW THE RULES
I doubt it This isn't some *fable.* And you're *not heroes.*
There aren't any heroes, not in the *real world.*
The next *morning* dawned crisp and cold, though it wouldn't stay that way for long.
Light your *arrows,* men!
Master Zo, what are you *doing?!*
The bandits are hiding in the *forest,* so I've decided to *burn it down.*

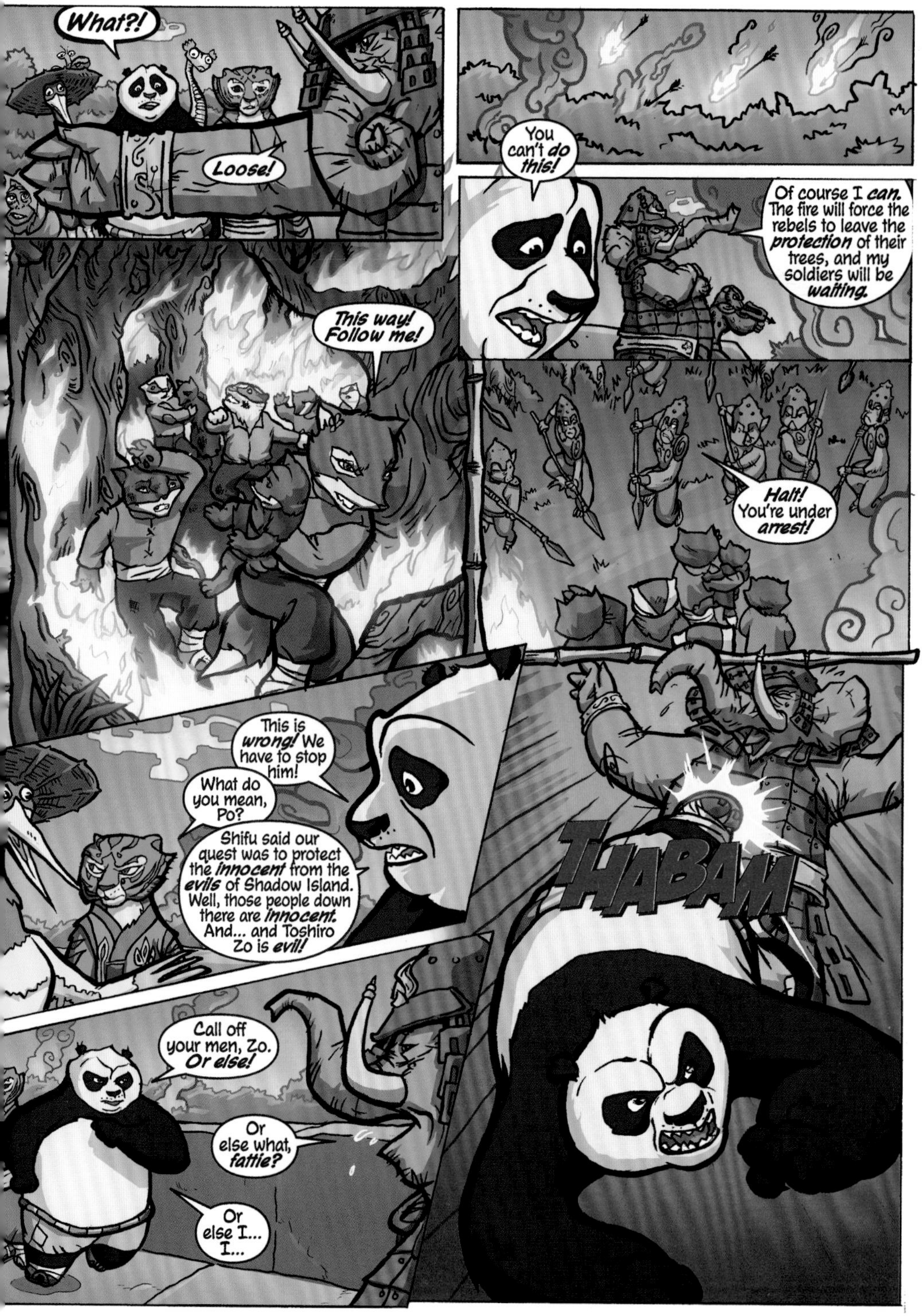
What?!
Loose!
You can't do this!
Of course I can. The fire will force the rebels to leave the protection of their trees, and my soldiers will be waiting.
This way! Follow me!
Halt! You're under arrest!
This is wrong! We have to stop him!
What do you mean, Po?
Shifu said our quest was to protect the innocent from the evils of Shadow Island. Well, those people down there are innocent. And... and Toshiro Zo is evil!
Call off your men, Zo. Or else!
Or else what, fattie?
Or else I... I...
THABAM

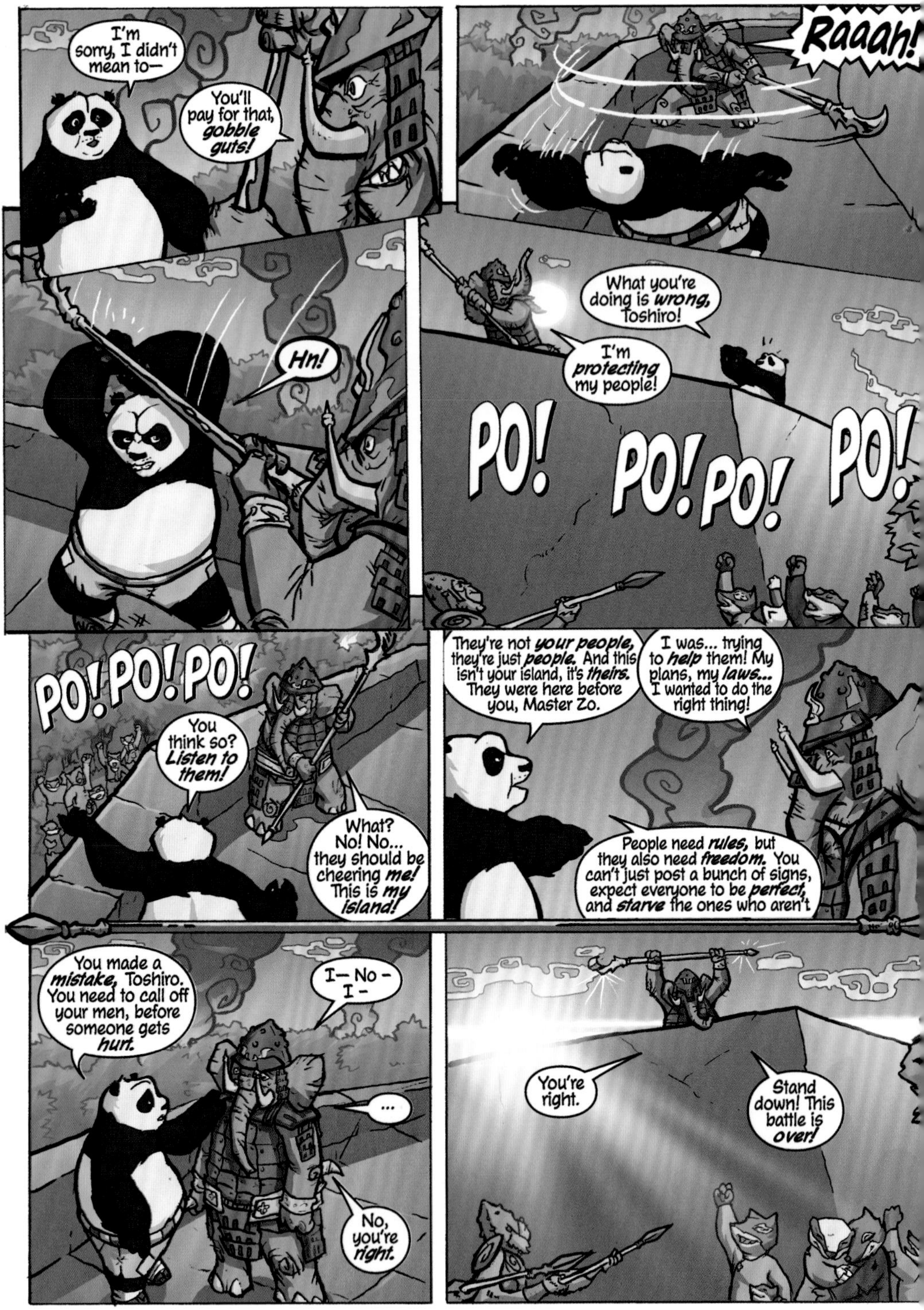
I'm sorry, I didn't mean to—
You'll pay for that, gobble guts!
Raaah!
Hn!
What you're doing is wrong, Toshiro!
I'm protecting my people!
PO! PO! PO! PO!
PO! PO! PO!
You think so? Listen to them!
What? No! No... they should be cheering me! This is my island!
They're not your people, they're just people. And this isn't your island, it's theirs. They were here before you, Master Zo.
I was... trying to help them! My plans, my laws... I wanted to do the right thing!
People need rules, but they also need freedom. You can't just post a bunch of signs, expect everyone to be perfect, and starve the ones who aren't
You made a mistake, Toshiro. You need to call off your men, before someone gets hurt.
I— No - I -
...
No, you're right.
You're right.
Stand down! This battle is over!

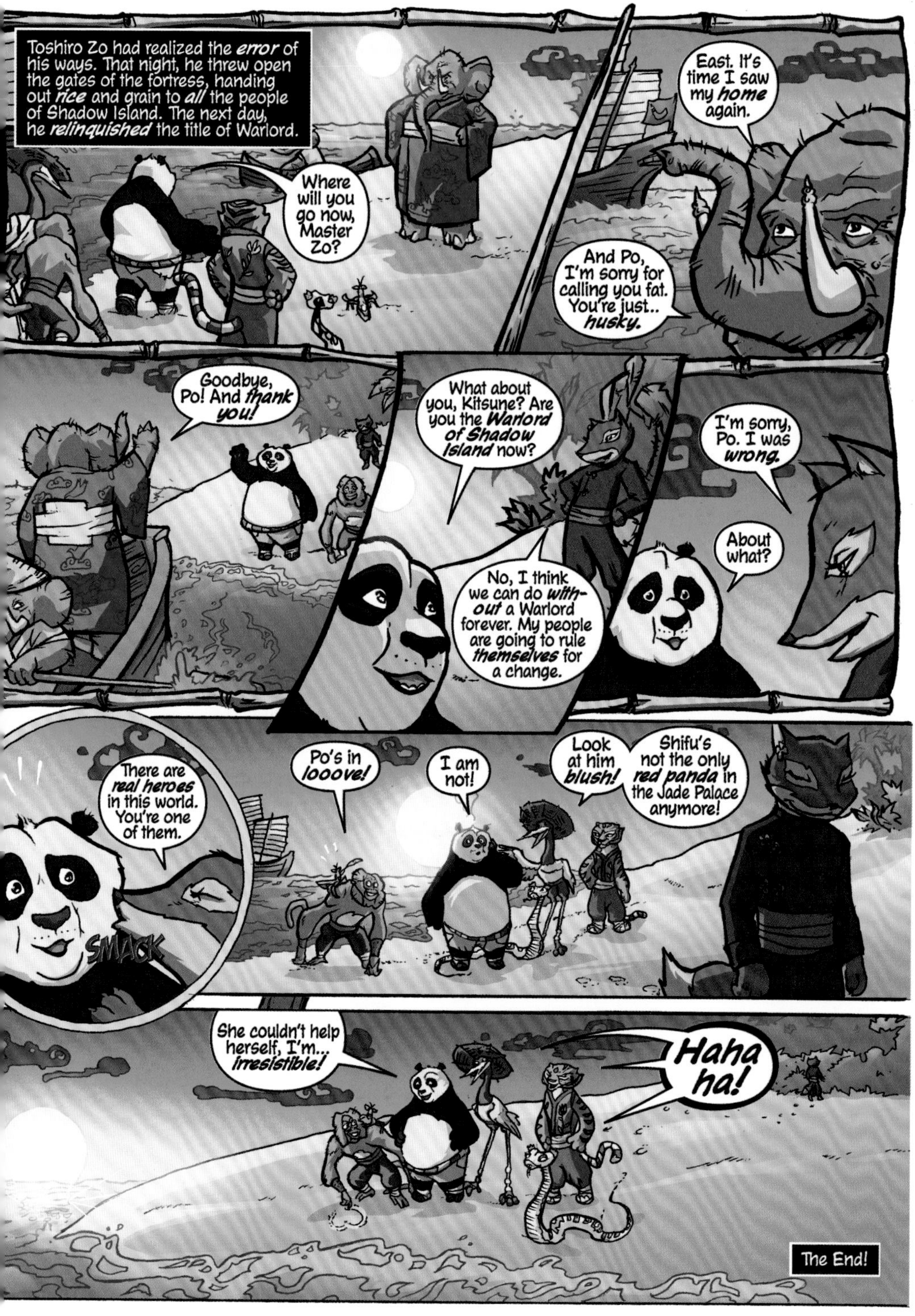
Toshiro Zo had realized the error of his ways. That night, he threw open the gates of the fortress, handing out rice and grain to all the people of Shadow Island. The next day, he relinquished the title of Warlord.
Where will you go now, Master Zo?
East. It's time I saw my home again.
And Po, I'm sorry for calling you fat. You're just.. husky.
Goodbye, Po! And thank you!
What about you, Kitsune? Are you the Warlord of Shadow Island now?
No, I think we can do without a Warlord forever. My people are going to rule themselves for a change.
I'm sorry, Po. I was wrong.
About what?
There are real heroes in this world. You're one of them.
SMACK
Po's in looove!
I am not!
Look at him blush!
Shifu's not the only red panda in the Jade Palace anymore!
She couldn't help herself, I'm... irresistible!
Haha ha!
The End!

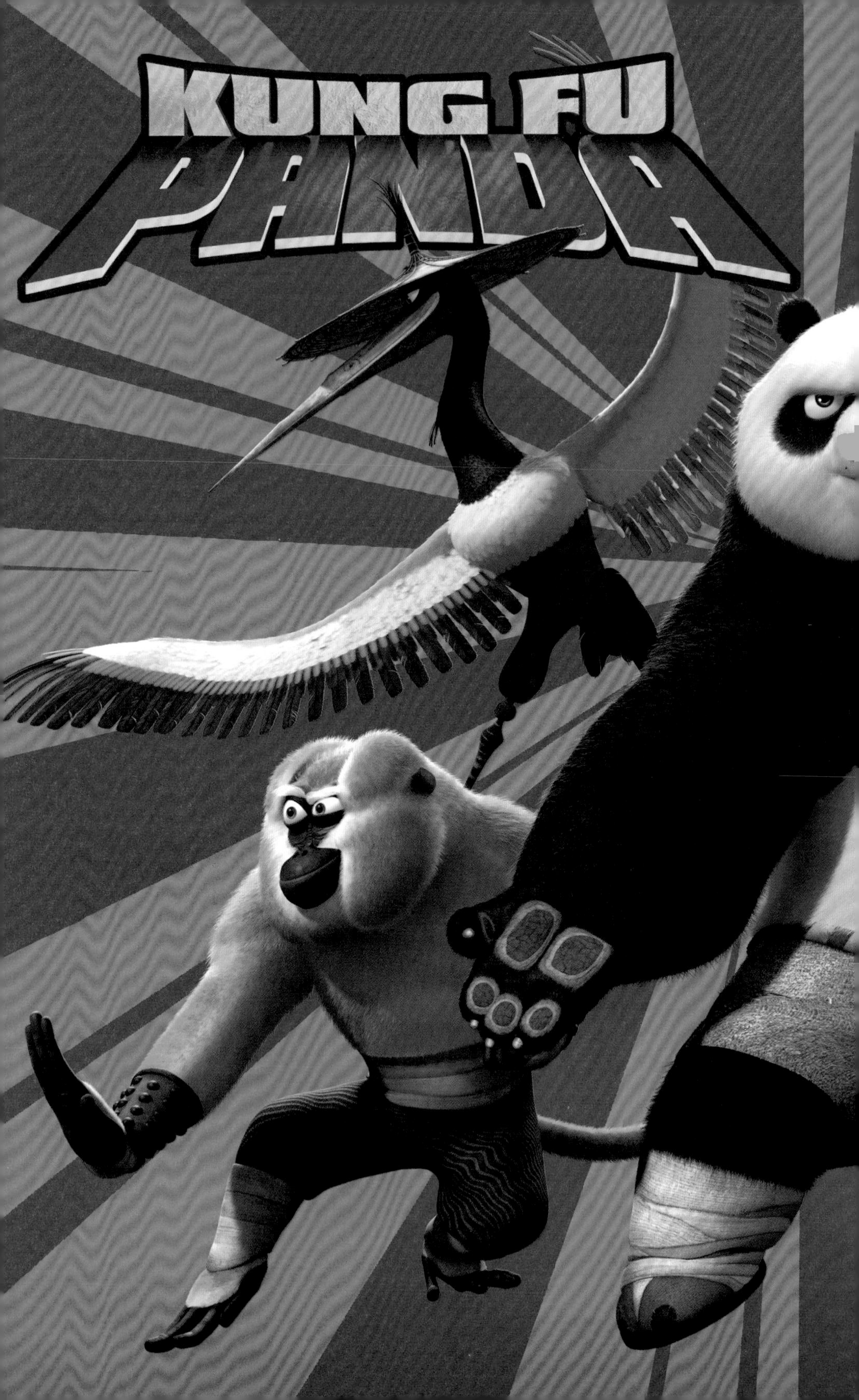
KUNG FU
PANDA

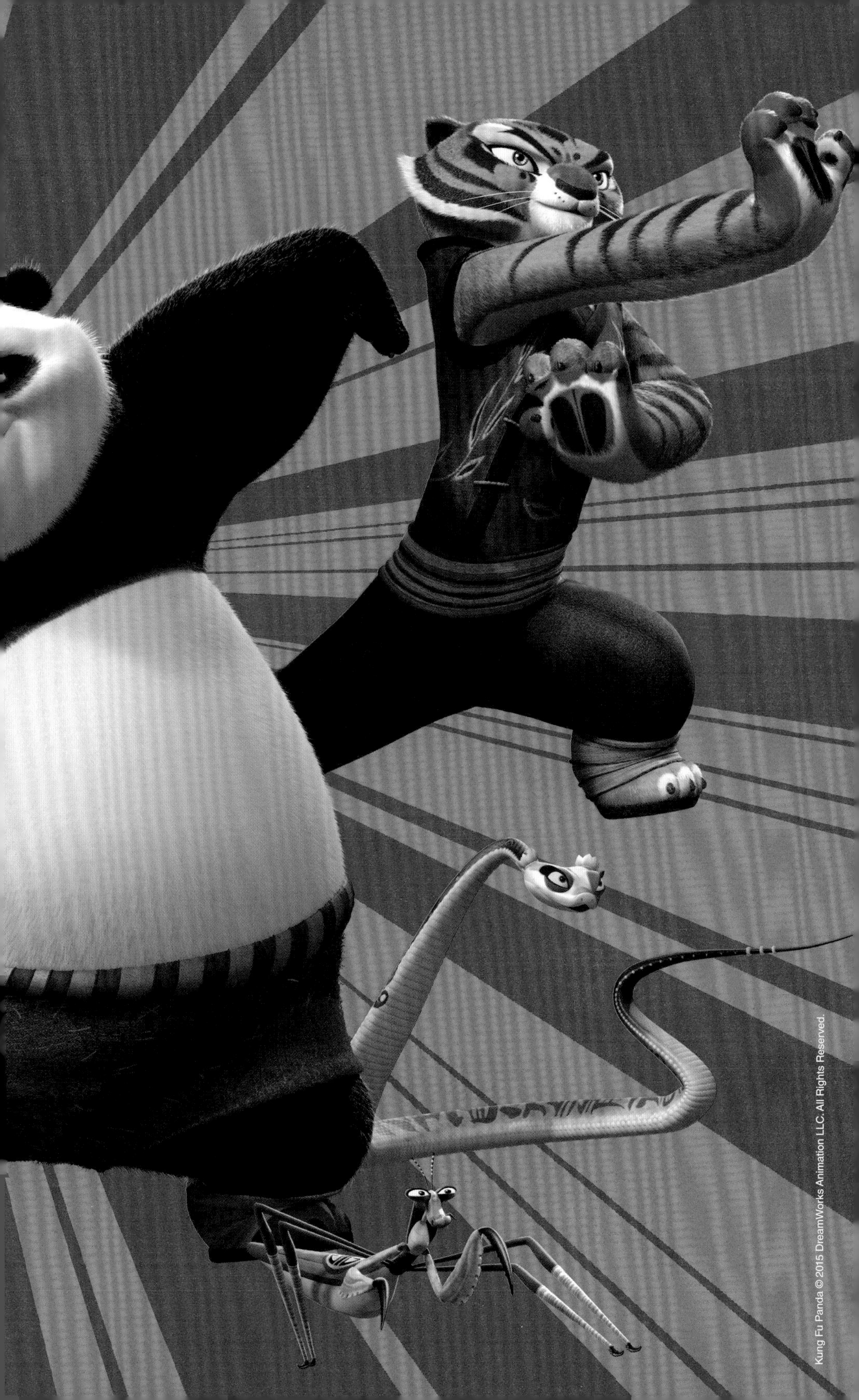

KUNG FU PANDA

VIPER

Master Viper is the "mother hen" of the group. It takes a cool head and warm heart to manage the personalities of the Furious Five. But don't let her gentle nature fool you. Viper is a lightning-fast warrior. Her power lies in her charm, her strength, he sinuous nature, her precision and in her deadly strike.

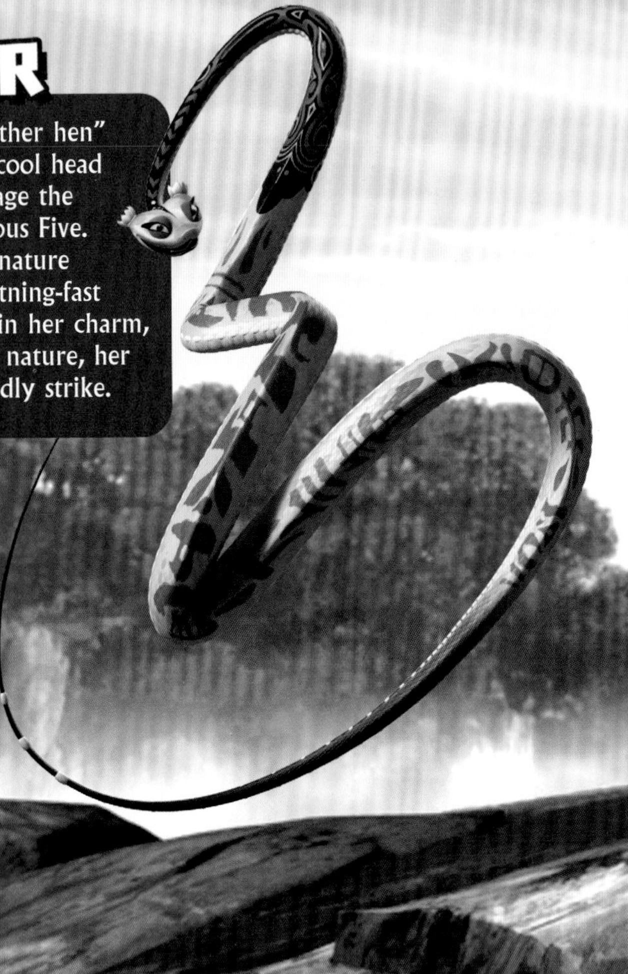

CRANE

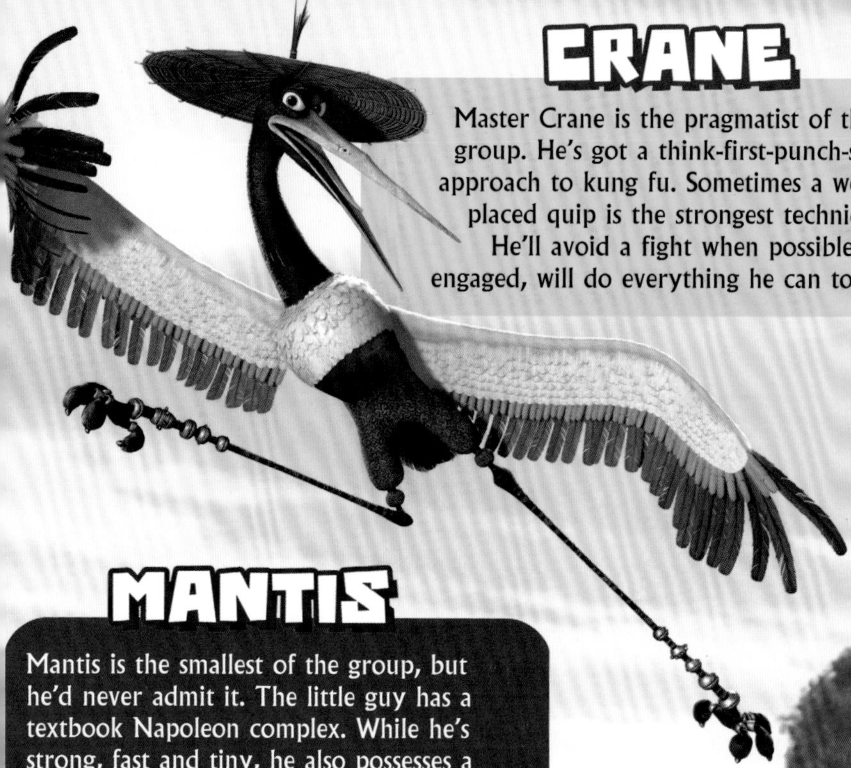

Master Crane is the pragmatist of the group. He's got a think-first-punch-second approach to kung fu. Sometimes a well-placed quip is the strongest technique. He'll avoid a fight when possible, but if engaged, will do everything he can to win.

MANTIS

Mantis is the smallest of the group, but he'd never admit it. The little guy has a textbook Napoleon complex. While he's strong, fast and tiny, he also possesses a mean temper and is ready to 'throw down' at the slightest insult. Nothing can strike fear into his brave little heart!

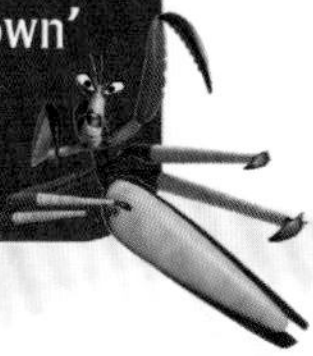

MR PING

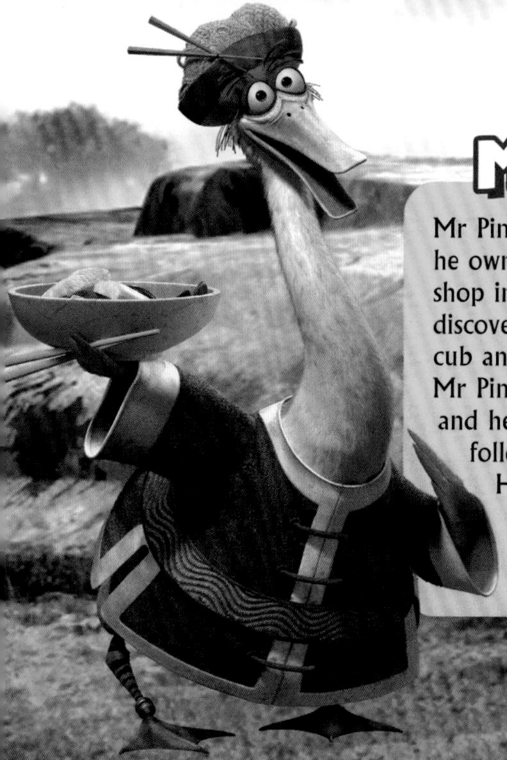

Mr Ping is Po's adoptive father, and he owns the most popular noodle shop in the Valley of Peace! Mr Ping discovered Po when he was a little cub and he adopted him soon after. Mr Ping's ancestors were noodle chefs and he was hoping that Po would follow him into the business. However, he has now accepted that Po's calling is to be the Dragon Warrior and he is proud of his son.

LET THE FUR FLY

WRITER **JASON M BURNS**
PENCILS **AURELIO MAZZARA**
COLORS **CV DESIGN**
LETTERS **DAVID HEDGECOCK**

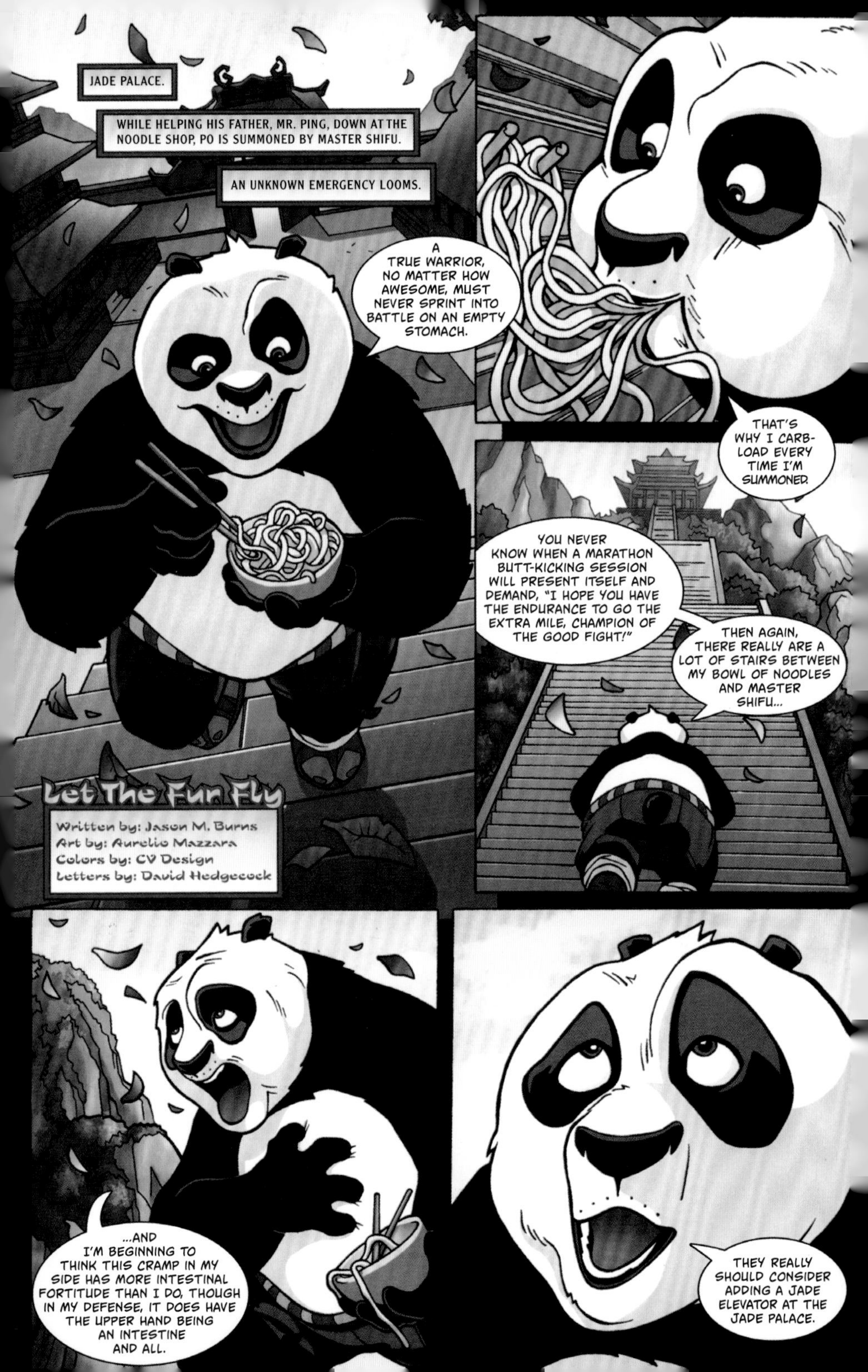

JADE PALACE.
WHILE HELPING HIS FATHER, MR. PING, DOWN AT THE NOODLE SHOP, PO IS SUMMONED BY MASTER SHIFU.
AN UNKNOWN EMERGENCY LOOMS.
A TRUE WARRIOR, NO MATTER HOW AWESOME, MUST NEVER SPRINT INTO BATTLE ON AN EMPTY STOMACH.
THAT'S WHY I CARB-LOAD EVERY TIME I'M SUMMONED.
Let The Fur Fly
Written by: Jason M. Burns
Art by: Aurelio Mazzara
Colors by: CV Design
Letters by: David Hedgecock
YOU NEVER KNOW WHEN A MARATHON BUTT-KICKING SESSION WILL PRESENT ITSELF AND DEMAND, "I HOPE YOU HAVE THE ENDURANCE TO GO THE EXTRA MILE, CHAMPION OF THE GOOD FIGHT!"
THEN AGAIN, THERE REALLY ARE A LOT OF STAIRS BETWEEN MY BOWL OF NOODLES AND MASTER SHIFU...
...AND I'M BEGINNING TO THINK THIS CRAMP IN MY SIDE HAS MORE INTESTINAL FORTITUDE THAN I DO, THOUGH IN MY DEFENSE, IT DOES HAVE THE UPPER HAND BEING AN INTESTINE AND ALL.
THEY REALLY SHOULD CONSIDER ADDING A JADE ELEVATOR AT THE JADE PALACE.

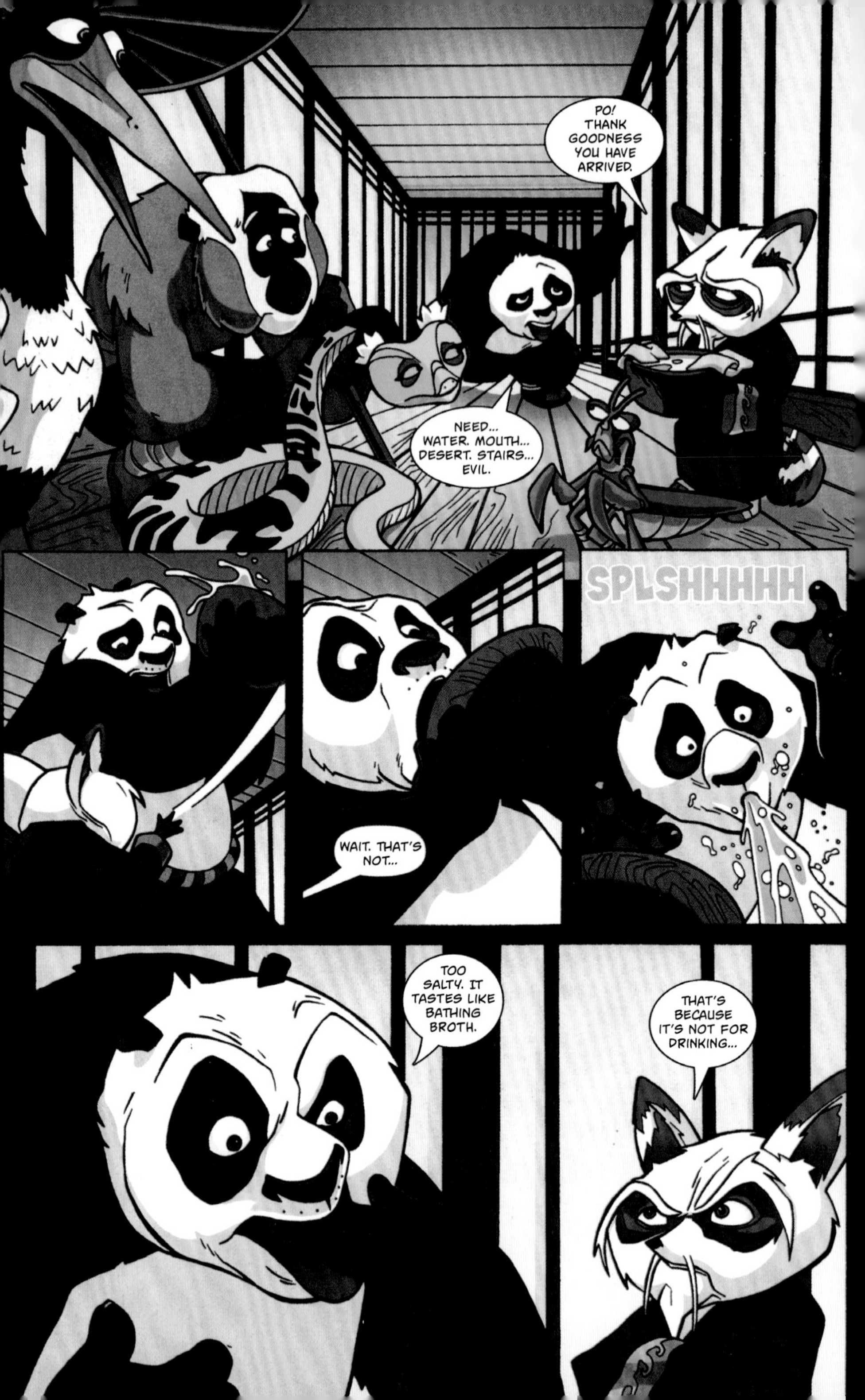
PO! THANK GOODNESS YOU HAVE ARRIVED.
NEED... WATER. MOUTH... DESERT. STAIRS... EVIL.
WAIT. THAT'S NOT...
SPLSHHHHH
TOO SALTY. IT TASTES LIKE BATHING BROTH.
THAT'S BECAUSE IT'S NOT FOR DRINKING...

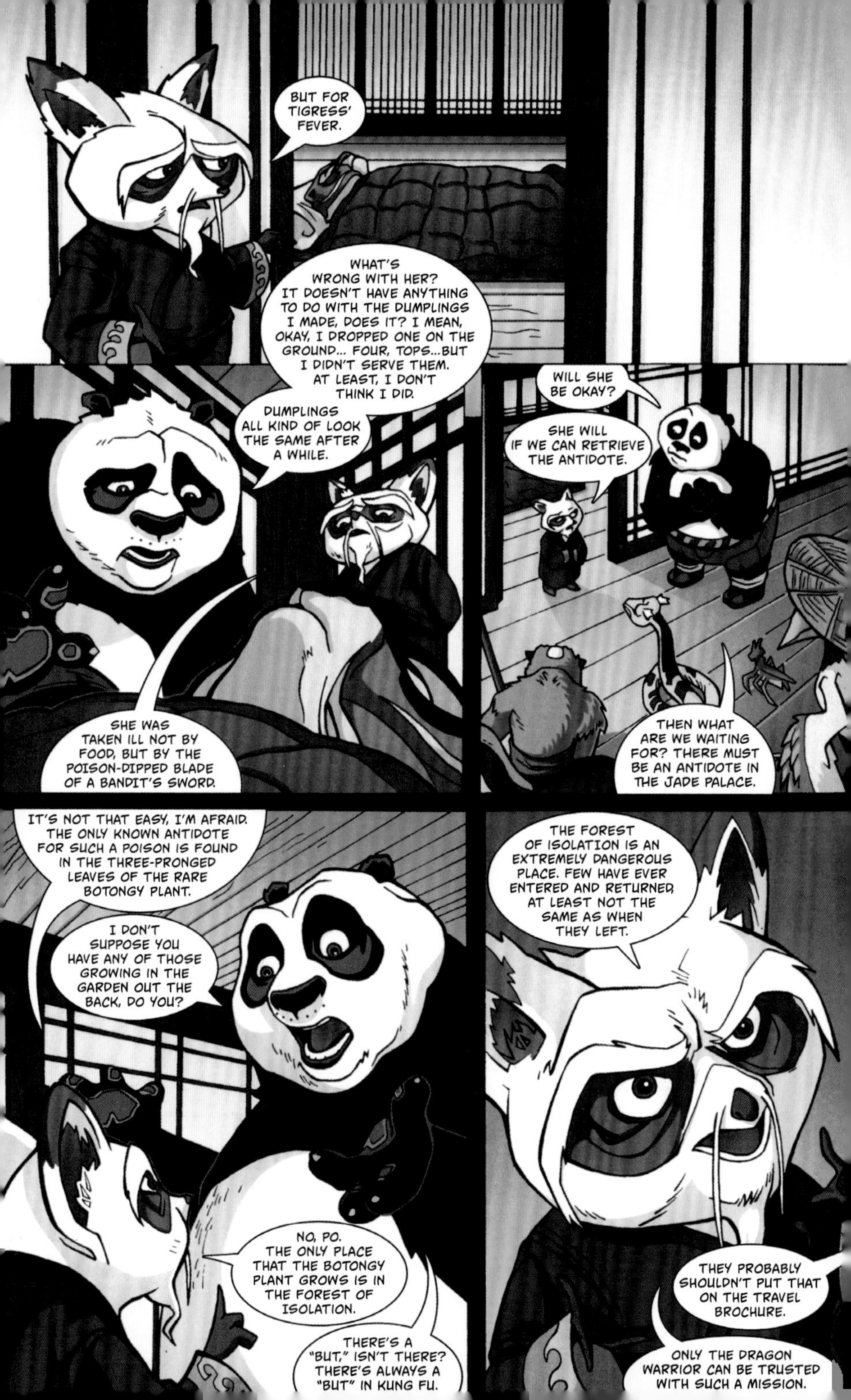
BUT FOR TIGRESS' FEVER.
WHAT'S WRONG WITH HER? IT DOESN'T HAVE ANYTHING TO DO WITH THE DUMPLINGS I MADE, DOES IT? I MEAN, OKAY, I DROPPED ONE ON THE GROUND... FOUR, TOPS...BUT I DIDN'T SERVE THEM. AT LEAST, I DON'T THINK I DID.
DUMPLINGS ALL KIND OF LOOK THE SAME AFTER A WHILE.
SHE WAS TAKEN ILL NOT BY FOOD, BUT BY THE POISON-DIPPED BLADE OF A BANDIT'S SWORD.
WILL SHE BE OKAY?
SHE WILL IF WE CAN RETRIEVE THE ANTIDOTE.
THEN WHAT ARE WE WAITING FOR? THERE MUST BE AN ANTIDOTE IN THE JADE PALACE.
IT'S NOT THAT EASY, I'M AFRAID. THE ONLY KNOWN ANTIDOTE FOR SUCH A POISON IS FOUND IN THE THREE-PRONGED LEAVES OF THE RARE BOTONGY PLANT.
I DON'T SUPPOSE YOU HAVE ANY OF THOSE GROWING IN THE GARDEN OUT THE BACK, DO YOU?
NO, PO. THE ONLY PLACE THAT THE BOTONGY PLANT GROWS IS IN THE FOREST OF ISOLATION.
THERE'S A "BUT," ISN'T THERE? THERE'S ALWAYS A "BUT" IN KUNG FU.
THE FOREST OF ISOLATION IS AN EXTREMELY DANGEROUS PLACE. FEW HAVE EVER ENTERED AND RETURNED, AT LEAST NOT THE SAME AS WHEN THEY LEFT.
THEY PROBABLY SHOULDN'T PUT THAT ON THE TRAVEL BROCHURE.
ONLY THE DRAGON WARRIOR CAN BE TRUSTED WITH SUCH A MISSION.

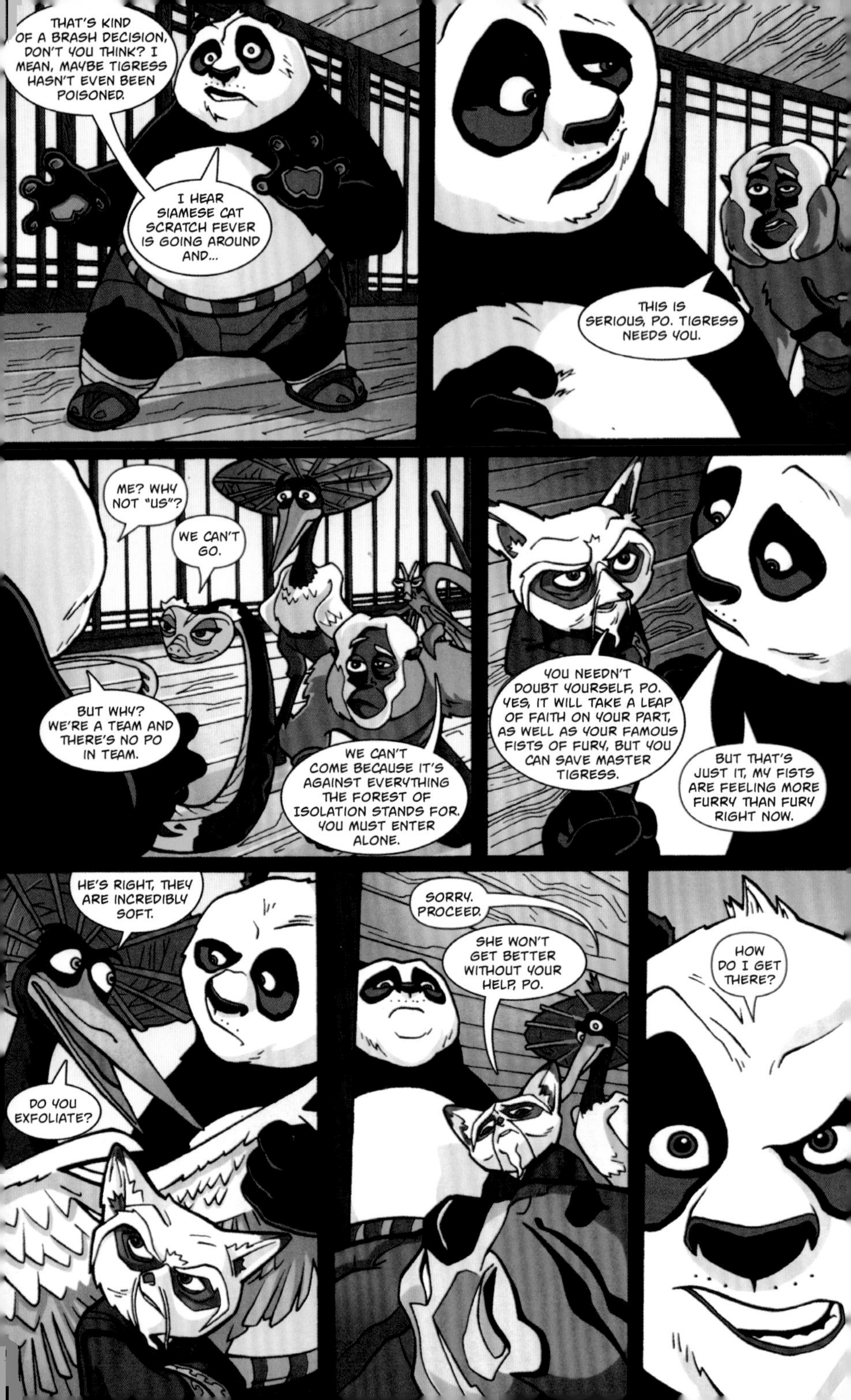
THAT'S KIND OF A BRASH DECISION, DON'T YOU THINK? I MEAN, MAYBE TIGRESS HASN'T EVEN BEEN POISONED.
I HEAR SIAMESE CAT SCRATCH FEVER IS GOING AROUND AND...
THIS IS SERIOUS, PO. TIGRESS NEEDS YOU.
ME? WHY NOT "US"?
WE CAN'T GO.
BUT WHY? WE'RE A TEAM AND THERE'S NO PO IN TEAM.
WE CAN'T COME BECAUSE IT'S AGAINST EVERYTHING THE FOREST OF ISOLATION STANDS FOR. YOU MUST ENTER ALONE.
YOU NEEDN'T DOUBT YOURSELF, PO. YES, IT WILL TAKE A LEAP OF FAITH ON YOUR PART, AS WELL AS YOUR FAMOUS FISTS OF FURY, BUT YOU CAN SAVE MASTER TIGRESS.
BUT THAT'S JUST IT, MY FISTS ARE FEELING MORE FURRY THAN FURY RIGHT NOW.
HE'S RIGHT, THEY ARE INCREDIBLY SOFT.
DO YOU EXFOLIATE?
SORRY. PROCEED.
SHE WON'T GET BETTER WITHOUT YOUR HELP, PO.
HOW DO I GET THERE?

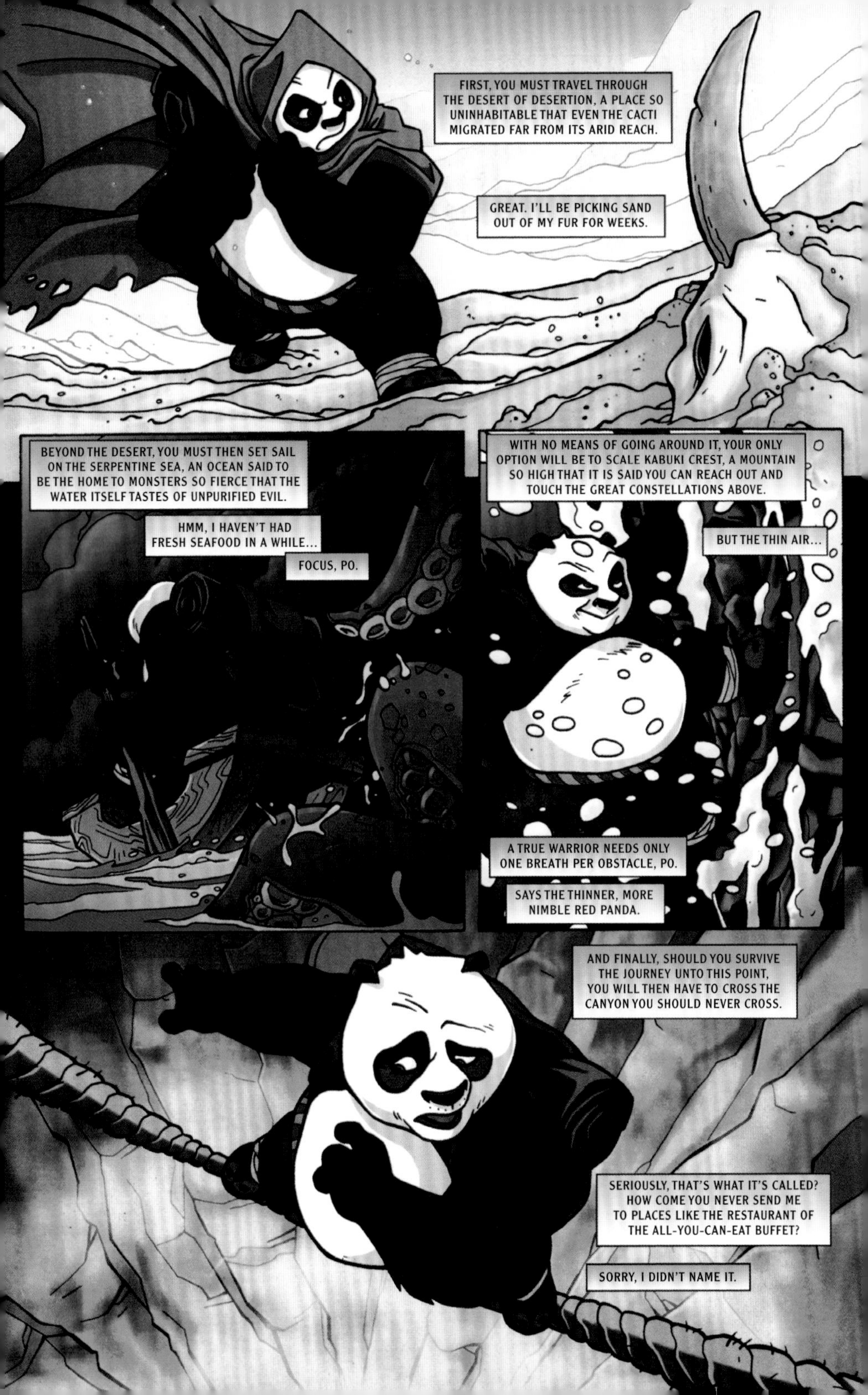
FIRST, YOU MUST TRAVEL THROUGH THE DESERT OF DESERTION, A PLACE SO UNINHABITABLE THAT EVEN THE CACTI MIGRATED FAR FROM ITS ARID REACH.
GREAT. I'LL BE PICKING SAND OUT OF MY FUR FOR WEEKS.
BEYOND THE DESERT, YOU MUST THEN SET SAIL ON THE SERPENTINE SEA, AN OCEAN SAID TO BE THE HOME TO MONSTERS SO FIERCE THAT THE WATER ITSELF TASTES OF UNPURIFIED EVIL.
HMM, I HAVEN'T HAD FRESH SEAFOOD IN A WHILE...
FOCUS, PO.
WITH NO MEANS OF GOING AROUND IT, YOUR ONLY OPTION WILL BE TO SCALE KABUKI CREST, A MOUNTAIN SO HIGH THAT IT IS SAID YOU CAN REACH OUT AND TOUCH THE GREAT CONSTELLATIONS ABOVE.
BUT THE THIN AIR...
A TRUE WARRIOR NEEDS ONLY ONE BREATH PER OBSTACLE, PO.
SAYS THE THINNER, MORE NIMBLE RED PANDA.
AND FINALLY, SHOULD YOU SURVIVE THE JOURNEY UNTO THIS POINT, YOU WILL THEN HAVE TO CROSS THE CANYON YOU SHOULD NEVER CROSS.
SERIOUSLY, THAT'S WHAT IT'S CALLED? HOW COME YOU NEVER SEND ME TO PLACES LIKE THE RESTAURANT OF THE ALL-YOU-CAN-EAT BUFFET?
SORRY, I DIDN'T NAME IT.

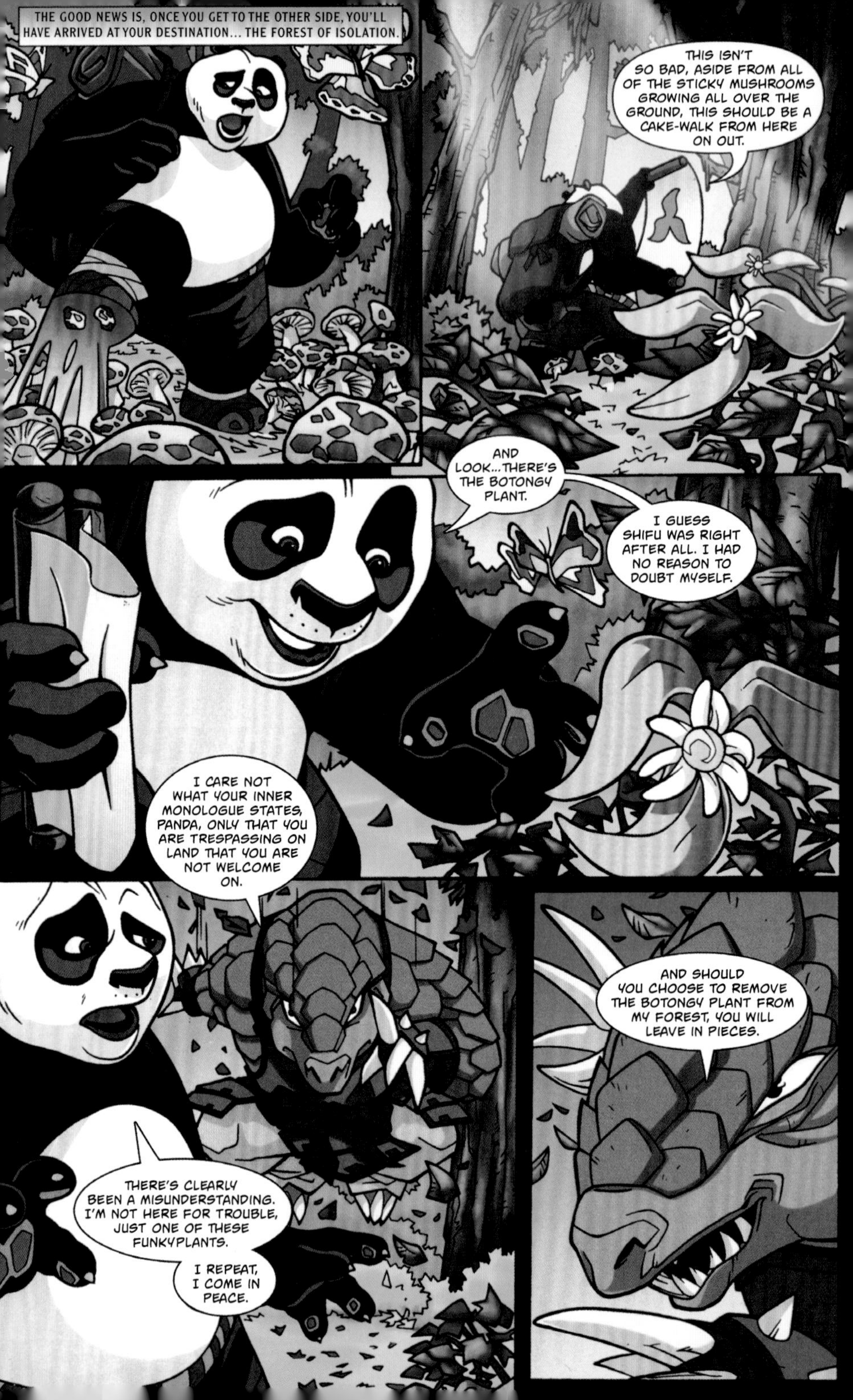
THE GOOD NEWS IS, ONCE YOU GET TO THE OTHER SIDE, YOU'LL HAVE ARRIVED AT YOUR DESTINATION... THE FOREST OF ISOLATION.
THIS ISN'T SO BAD, ASIDE FROM ALL OF THE STICKY MUSHROOMS GROWING ALL OVER THE GROUND, THIS SHOULD BE A CAKE-WALK FROM HERE ON OUT.
AND LOOK...THERE'S THE BOTONGY PLANT.
I GUESS SHIFU WAS RIGHT AFTER ALL. I HAD NO REASON TO DOUBT MYSELF.
I CARE NOT WHAT YOUR INNER MONOLOGUE STATES, PANDA, ONLY THAT YOU ARE TRESPASSING ON LAND THAT YOU ARE NOT WELCOME ON.
THERE'S CLEARLY BEEN A MISUNDERSTANDING. I'M NOT HERE FOR TROUBLE, JUST ONE OF THESE FUNKYPLANTS.
I REPEAT, I COME IN PEACE.
AND SHOULD YOU CHOOSE TO REMOVE THE BOTONGY PLANT FROM MY FOREST, YOU WILL LEAVE IN PIECES.

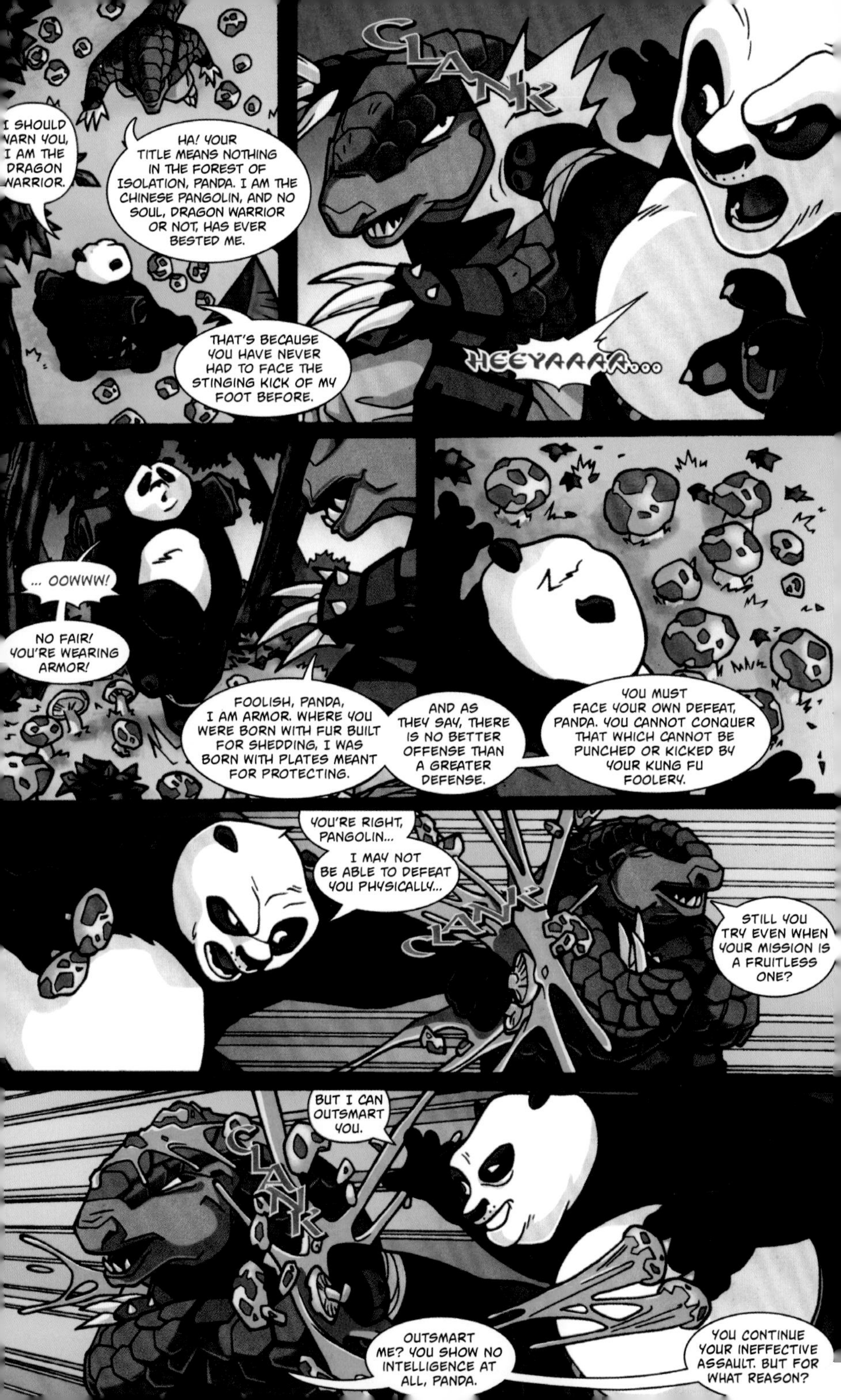

I SHOULD WARN YOU, I AM THE DRAGON WARRIOR.
HA! YOUR TITLE MEANS NOTHING IN THE FOREST OF ISOLATION, PANDA. I AM THE CHINESE PANGOLIN, AND NO SOUL, DRAGON WARRIOR OR NOT, HAS EVER BESTED ME.
THAT'S BECAUSE YOU HAVE NEVER HAD TO FACE THE STINGING KICK OF MY FOOT BEFORE.
CLANK
HEEYAAAA...
... OOWWW!
NO FAIR! YOU'RE WEARING ARMOR!
FOOLISH, PANDA, I AM ARMOR. WHERE YOU WERE BORN WITH FUR BUILT FOR SHEDDING, I WAS BORN WITH PLATES MEANT FOR PROTECTING.
AND AS THEY SAY, THERE IS NO BETTER OFFENSE THAN A GREATER DEFENSE.
YOU MUST FACE YOUR OWN DEFEAT, PANDA. YOU CANNOT CONQUER THAT WHICH CANNOT BE PUNCHED OR KICKED BY YOUR KUNG FU FOOLERY.
YOU'RE RIGHT, PANGOLIN...
I MAY NOT BE ABLE TO DEFEAT YOU PHYSICALLY...
CLANK
STILL YOU TRY EVEN WHEN YOUR MISSION IS A FRUITLESS ONE?
BUT I CAN OUTSMART YOU.
CLANK
OUTSMART ME? YOU SHOW NO INTELLIGENCE AT ALL, PANDA.
YOU CONTINUE YOUR INEFFECTIVE ASSAULT. BUT FOR WHAT REASON?

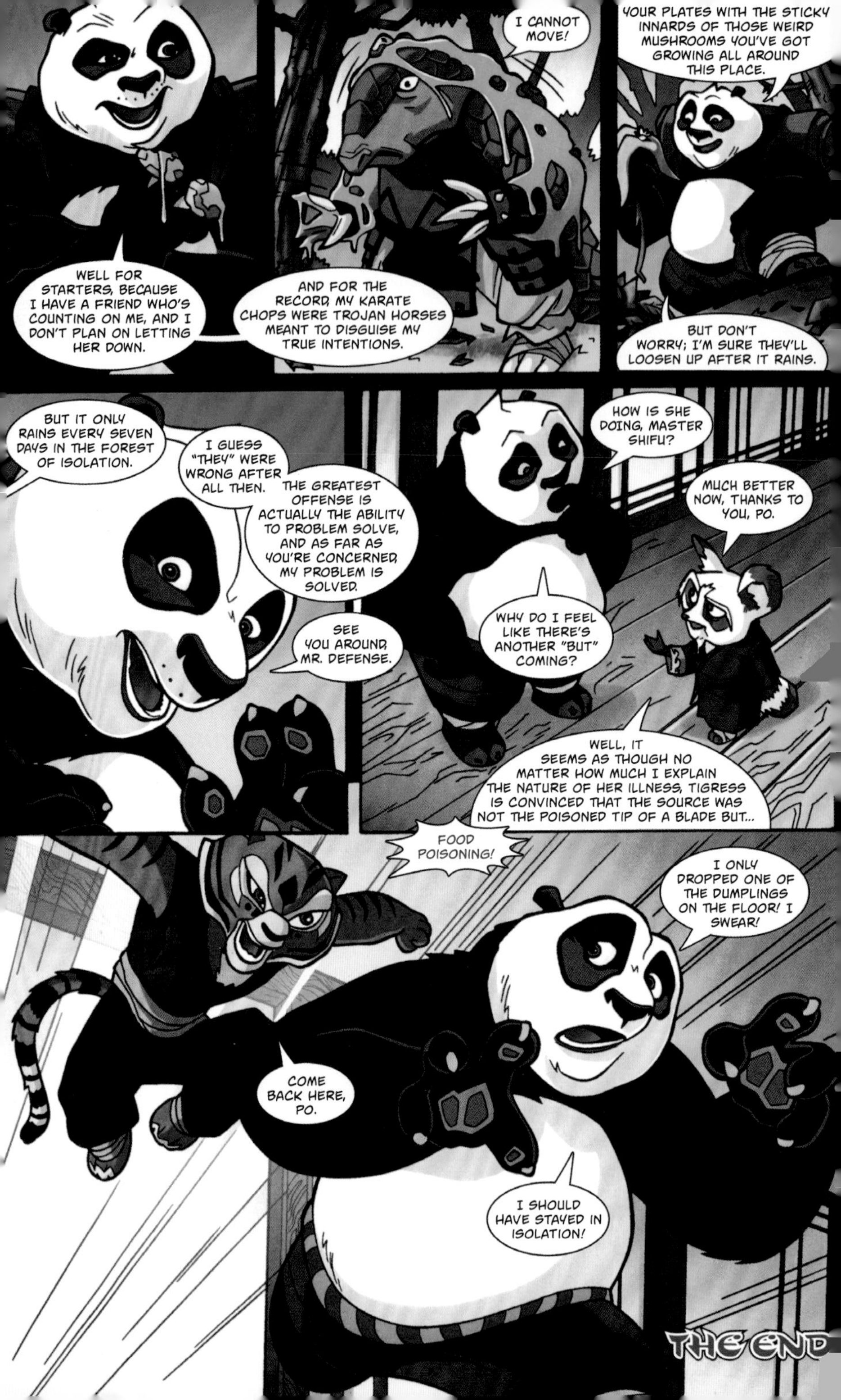

WELL FOR STARTERS, BECAUSE I HAVE A FRIEND WHO'S COUNTING ON ME, AND I DON'T PLAN ON LETTING HER DOWN.
I CANNOT MOVE!
AND FOR THE RECORD, MY KARATE CHOPS WERE TROJAN HORSES MEANT TO DISGUISE MY TRUE INTENTIONS.
YOUR PLATES WITH THE STICKY INNARDS OF THOSE WEIRD MUSHROOMS YOU'VE GOT GROWING ALL AROUND THIS PLACE.
BUT DON'T WORRY; I'M SURE THEY'LL LOOSEN UP AFTER IT RAINS.
BUT IT ONLY RAINS EVERY SEVEN DAYS IN THE FOREST OF ISOLATION.
I GUESS "THEY" WERE WRONG AFTER ALL THEN.
THE GREATEST OFFENSE IS ACTUALLY THE ABILITY TO PROBLEM SOLVE, AND AS FAR AS YOU'RE CONCERNED, MY PROBLEM IS SOLVED.
SEE YOU AROUND, MR. DEFENSE.
HOW IS SHE DOING, MASTER SHIFU?
MUCH BETTER NOW, THANKS TO YOU, PO.
WHY DO I FEEL LIKE THERE'S ANOTHER "BUT" COMING?
WELL, IT SEEMS AS THOUGH NO MATTER HOW MUCH I EXPLAIN THE NATURE OF HER ILLNESS, TIGRESS IS CONVINCED THAT THE SOURCE WAS NOT THE POISONED TIP OF A BLADE BUT...
FOOD POISONING!
I ONLY DROPPED ONE OF THE DUMPLINGS ON THE FLOOR! I SWEAR!
COME BACK HERE, PO.
I SHOULD HAVE STAYED IN ISOLATION!
THE END

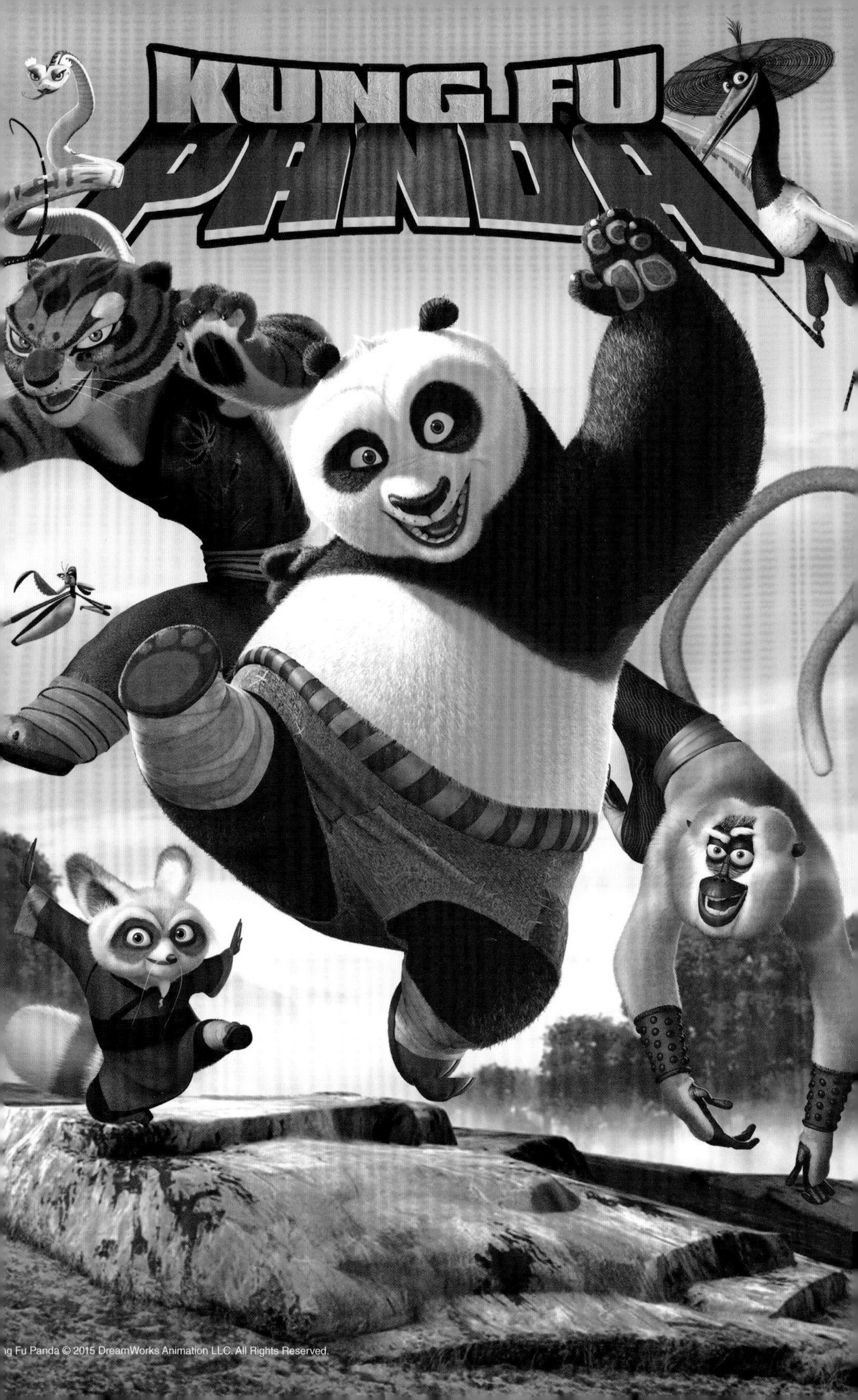
KUNG FU
PANDA

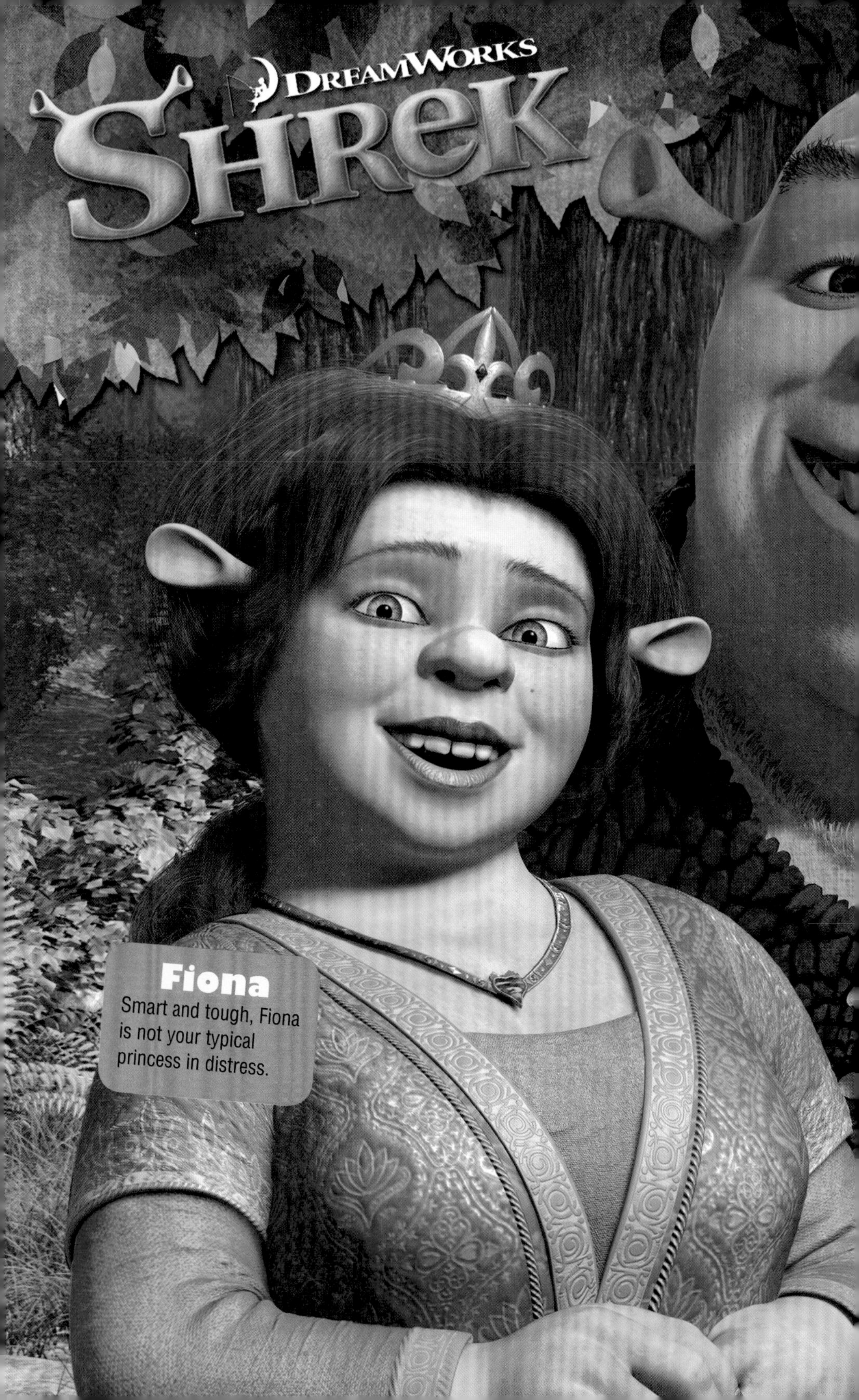
DreamWorks
Shrek
Fiona
Smart and tough, Fiona is not your typical princess in distress.

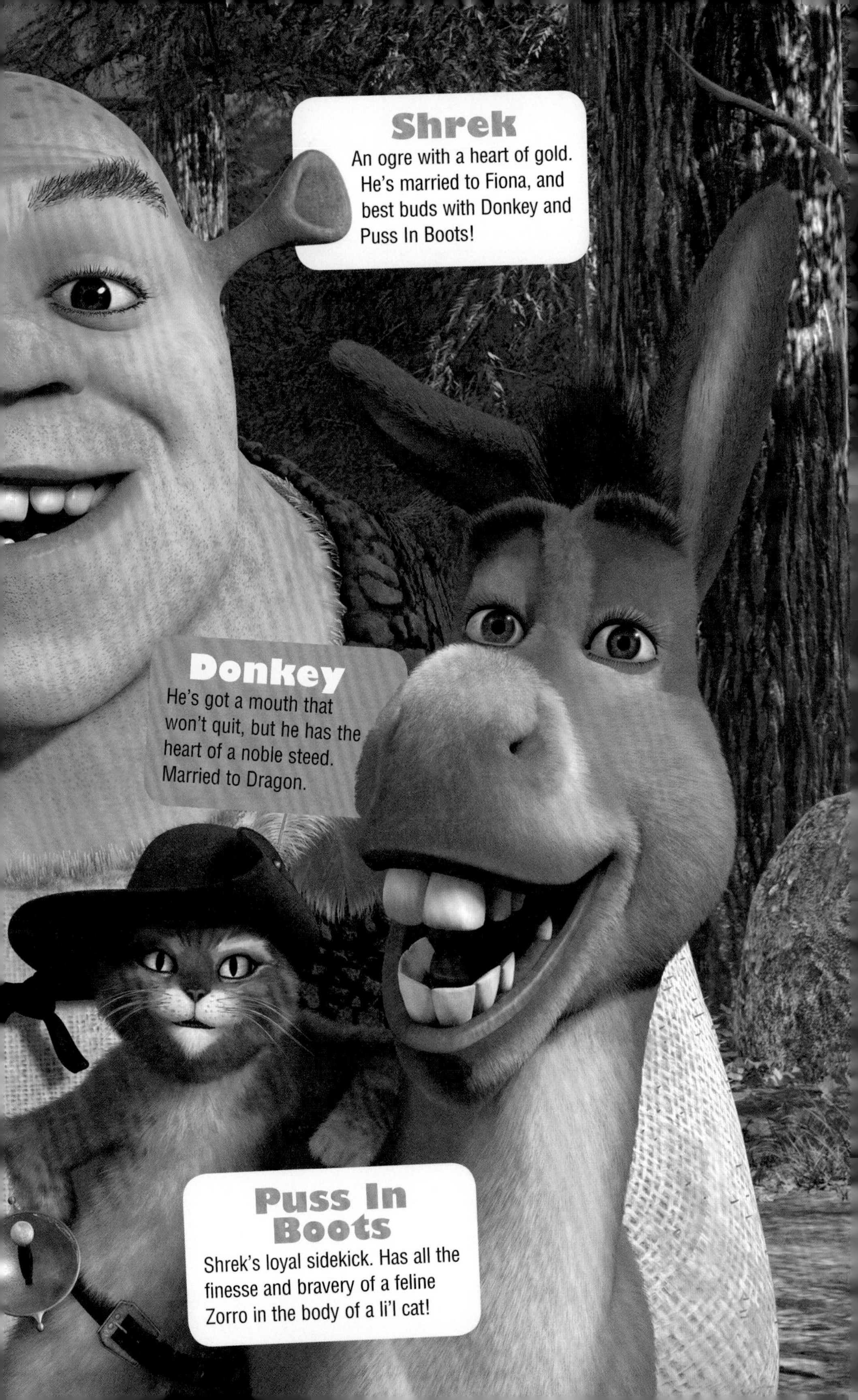

Shrek

An ogre with a heart of gold. He's married to Fiona, and best buds with Donkey and Puss In Boots!

Donkey

He's got a mouth that won't quit, but he has the heart of a noble steed. Married to Dragon.

Puss In Boots

Shrek's loyal sidekick. Has all the finesse and bravery of a feline Zorro in the body of a li'l cat!

DONKEY RIDE

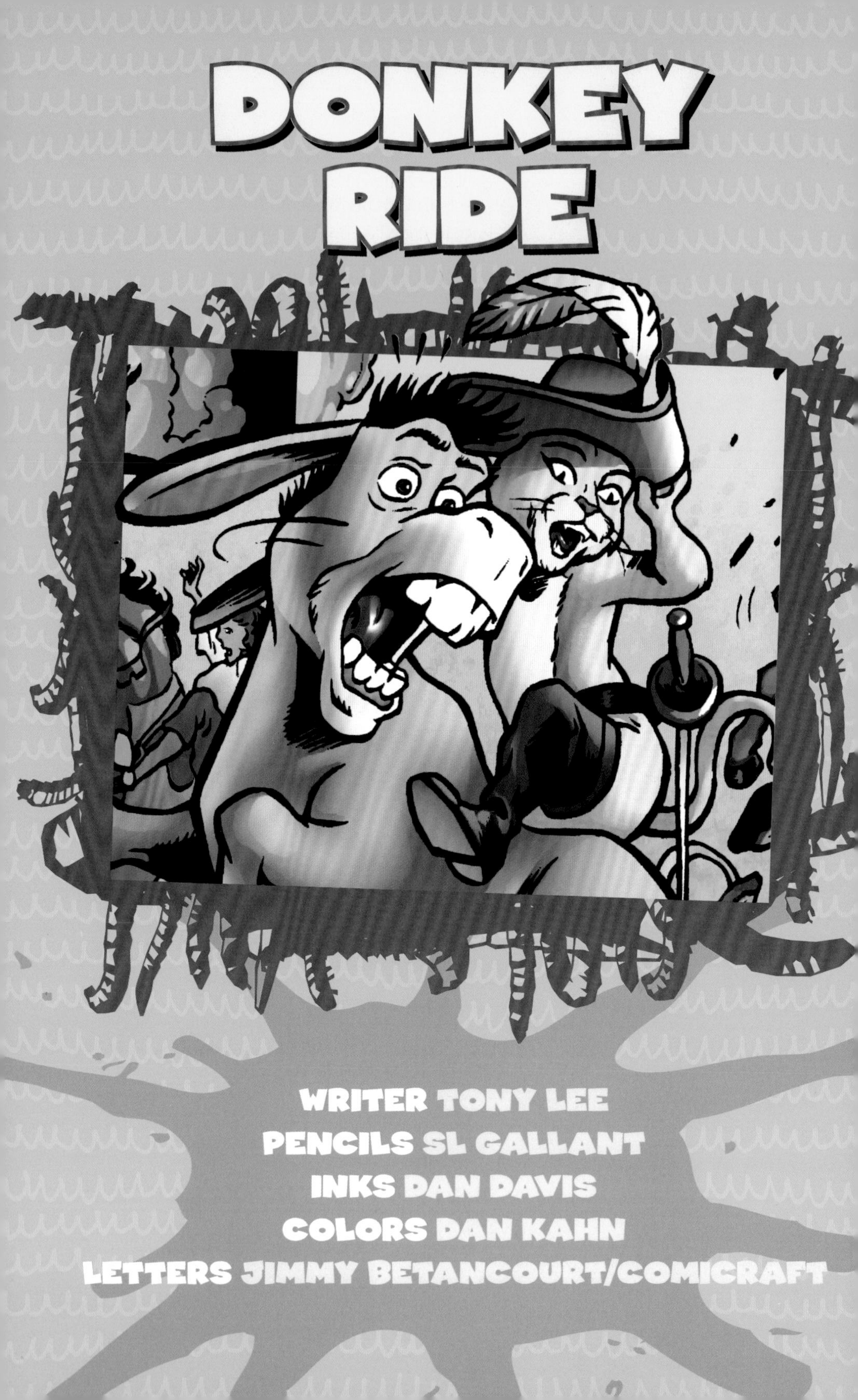

WRITER TONY LEE
PENCILS SL GALLANT
INKS DAN DAVIS
COLORS DAN KAHN
LETTERS JIMMY BETANCOURT/COMICRAFT

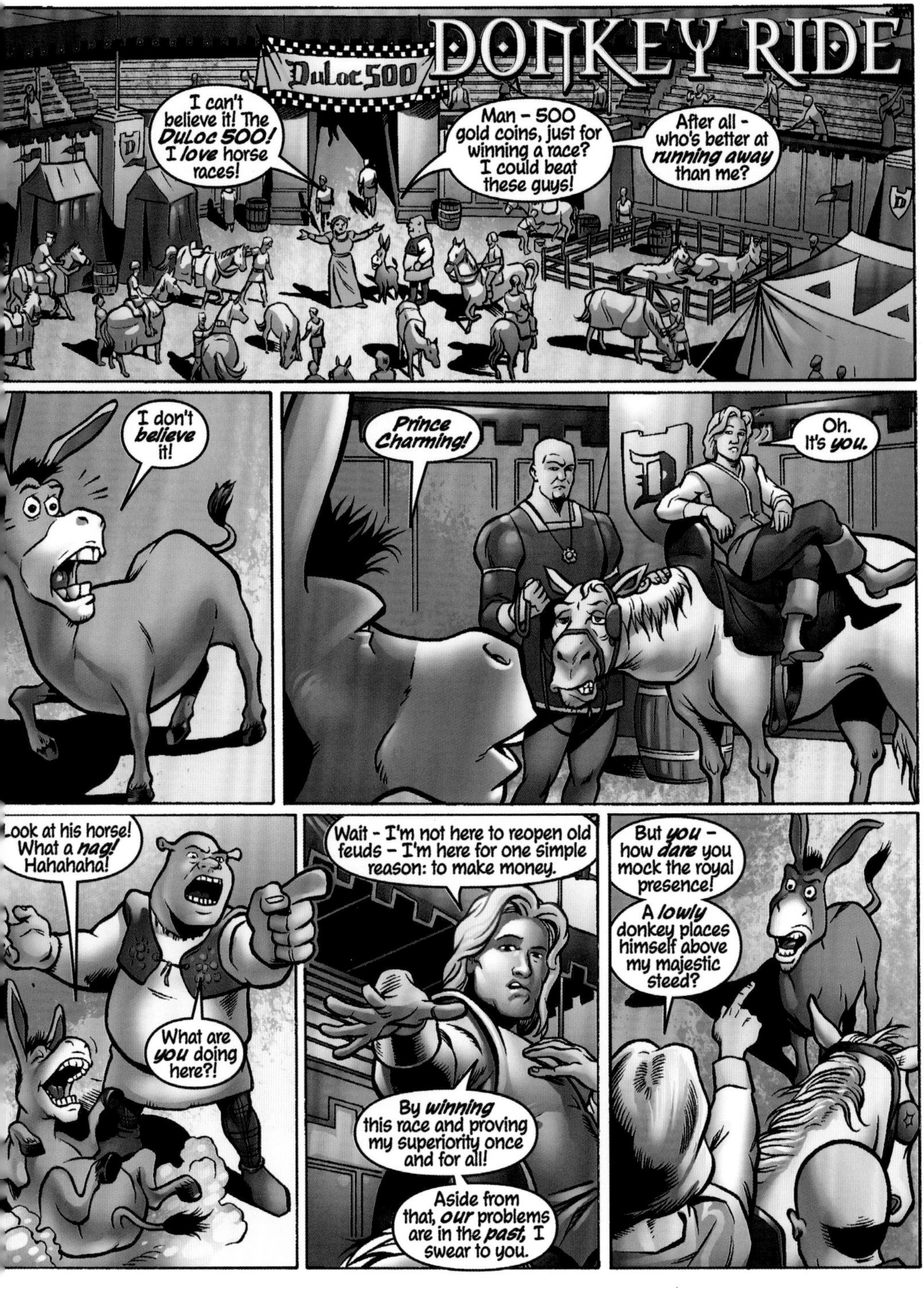
DONKEY RIDE
DuLoc 500
I can't believe it! The DuLoc 500! I love horse races!
Man - 500 gold coins, just for winning a race? I could beat these guys!
After all - who's better at running away than me?
I don't believe it!
Prince Charming!
Oh. It's you.
Look at his horse! What a nag! Hahahaha!
What are you doing here?!
Wait - I'm not here to reopen old feuds - I'm here for one simple reason: to make money.
By winning this race and proving my superiority once and for all!
Aside from that, our problems are in the past, I swear to you.
But you - how dare you mock the royal presence!
A lowly donkey places himself above my majestic steed?

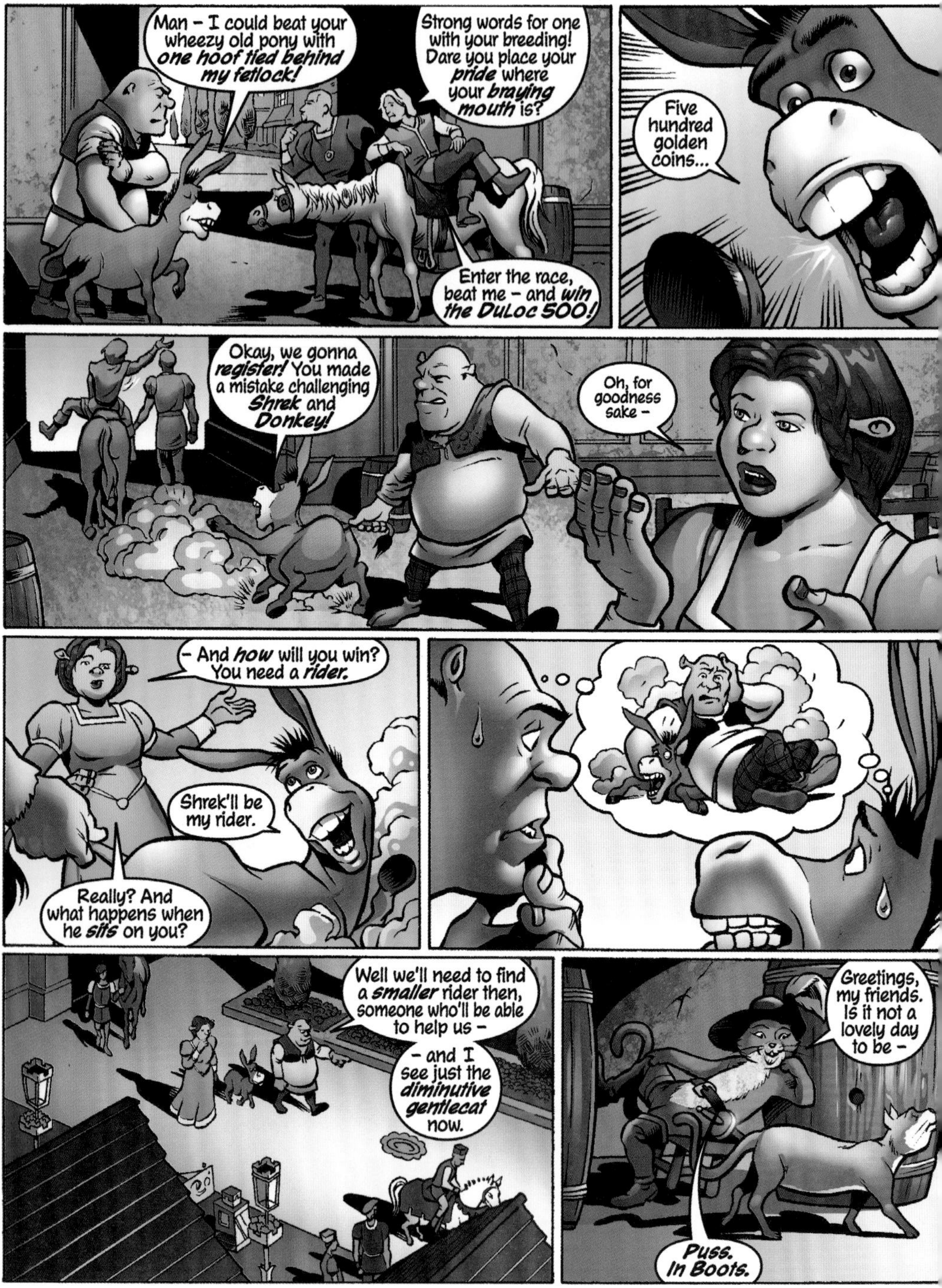
Man – I could beat your wheezy old pony with one hoof tied behind my fetlock!
Strong words for one with your breeding! Dare you place your pride where your braying mouth is?
Enter the race, beat me – and win the DuLoc 500!
Five hundred golden coins...
Okay, we gonna register! You made a mistake challenging Shrek and Donkey!
Oh, for goodness sake –
– And how will you win? You need a rider.
Shrek'll be my rider.
Really? And what happens when he sits on you?
Well we'll need to find a smaller rider then, someone who'll be able to help us –
– and I see just the diminutive gentlecat now.
Greetings, my friends. Is it not a lovely day to be –
Puss. In Boots.

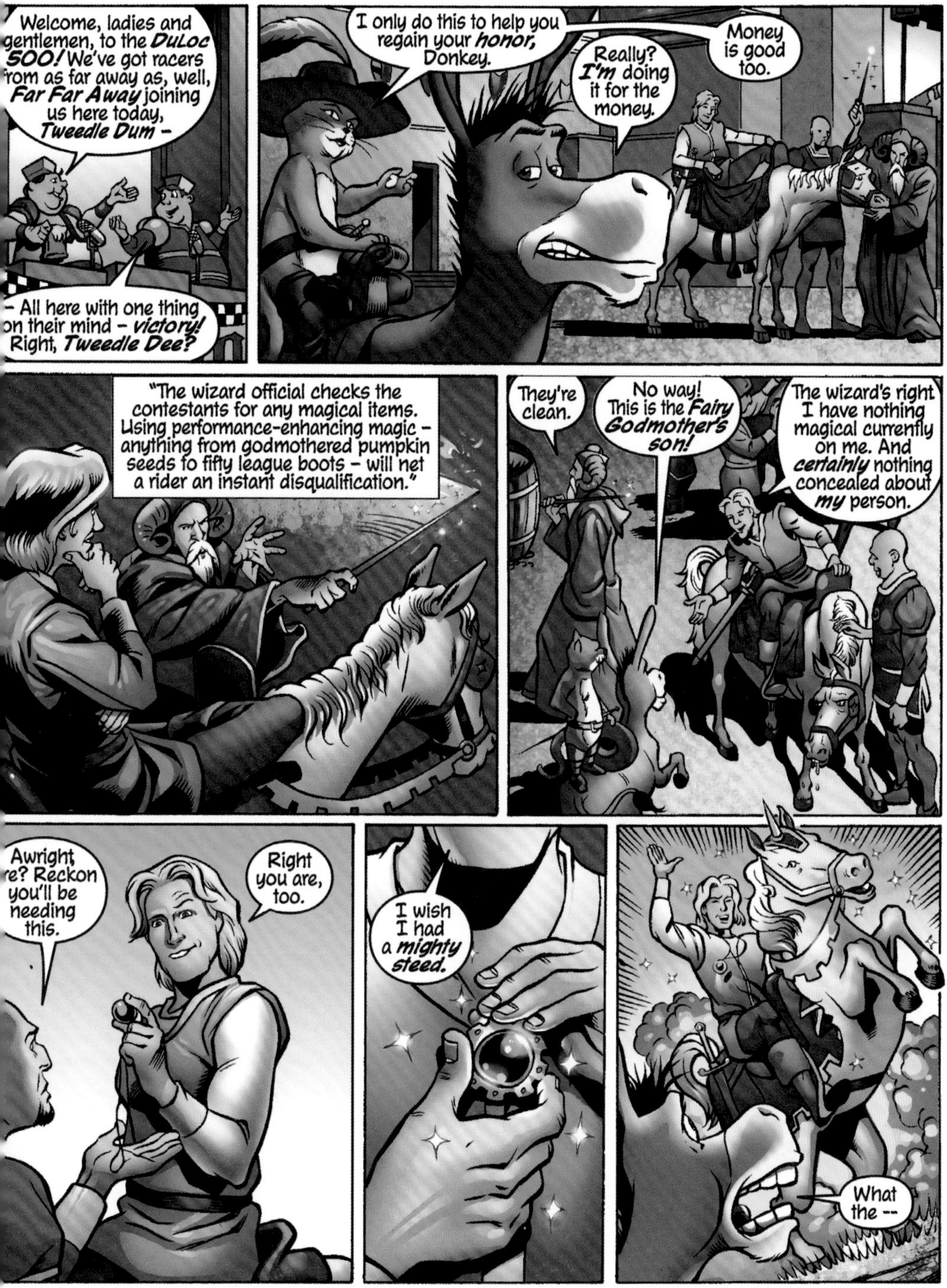
Welcome, ladies and gentlemen, to the DuLoc 500! We've got racers from as far away as, well, Far Far Away joining us here today, Tweedle Dum -
- All here with one thing on their mind - victory! Right, Tweedle Dee?
I only do this to help you regain your honor, Donkey.
Really? I'm doing it for the money.
Money is good too.
"The wizard official checks the contestants for any magical items. Using performance-enhancing magic - anything from godmothered pumpkin seeds to fifty league boots - will net a rider an instant disqualification."
They're clean.
No way! This is the Fairy Godmother's son!
The wizard's right I have nothing magical currently on me. And certainly nothing concealed about my person.
Awright re? Reckon you'll be needing this.
Right you are, too.
I wish I had a mighty steed.
What the --

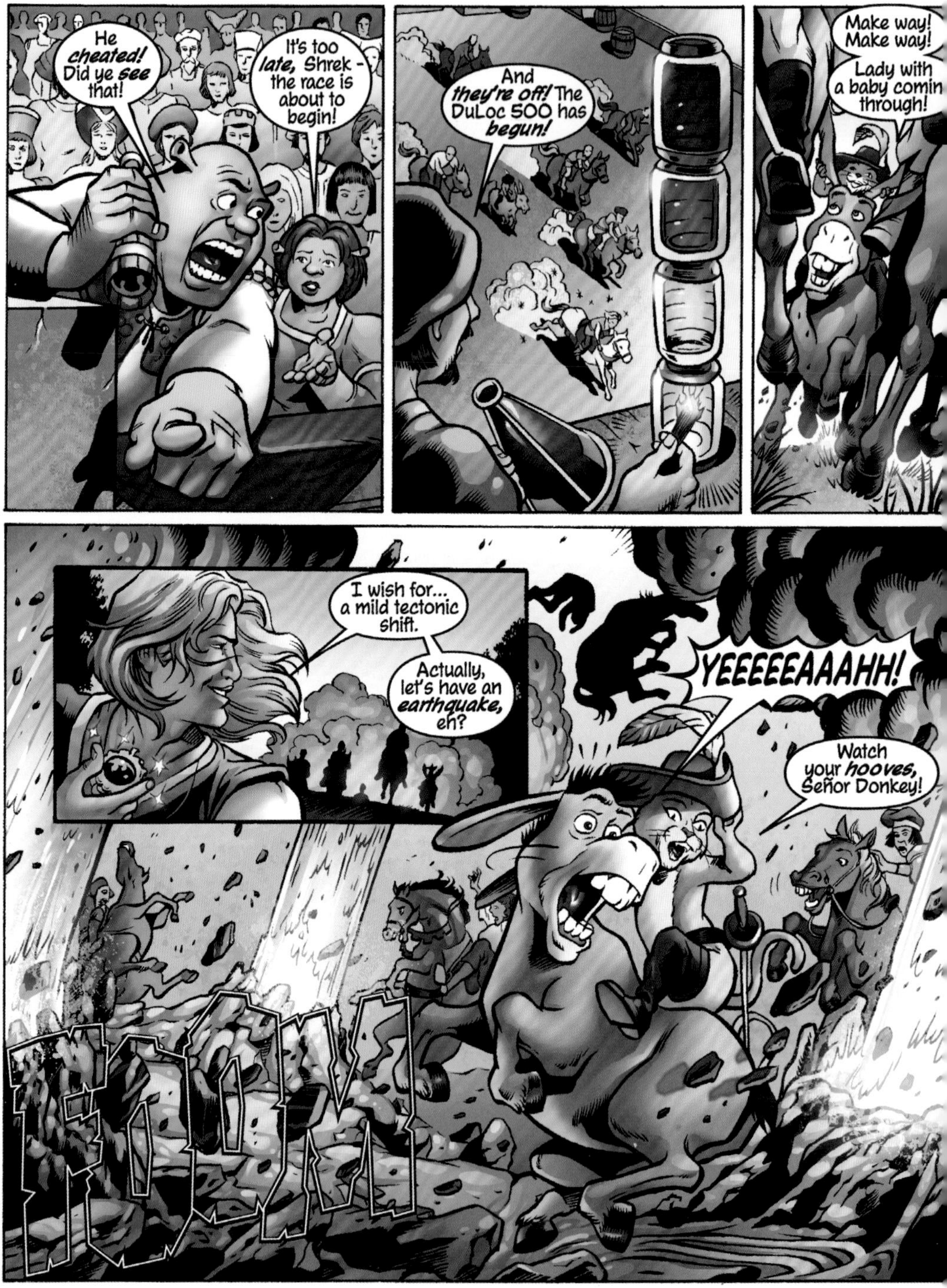
He cheated! Did ye see that!
It's too late, Shrek - the race is about to begin!
And they're off! The DuLoc 500 has begun!
Make way! Make way!
Lady with a baby comin through!
I wish for... a mild tectonic shift.
Actually, let's have an earthquake, eh?
YEEEEEAAAHH!
Watch your hooves, Señor Donkey!
FOOM

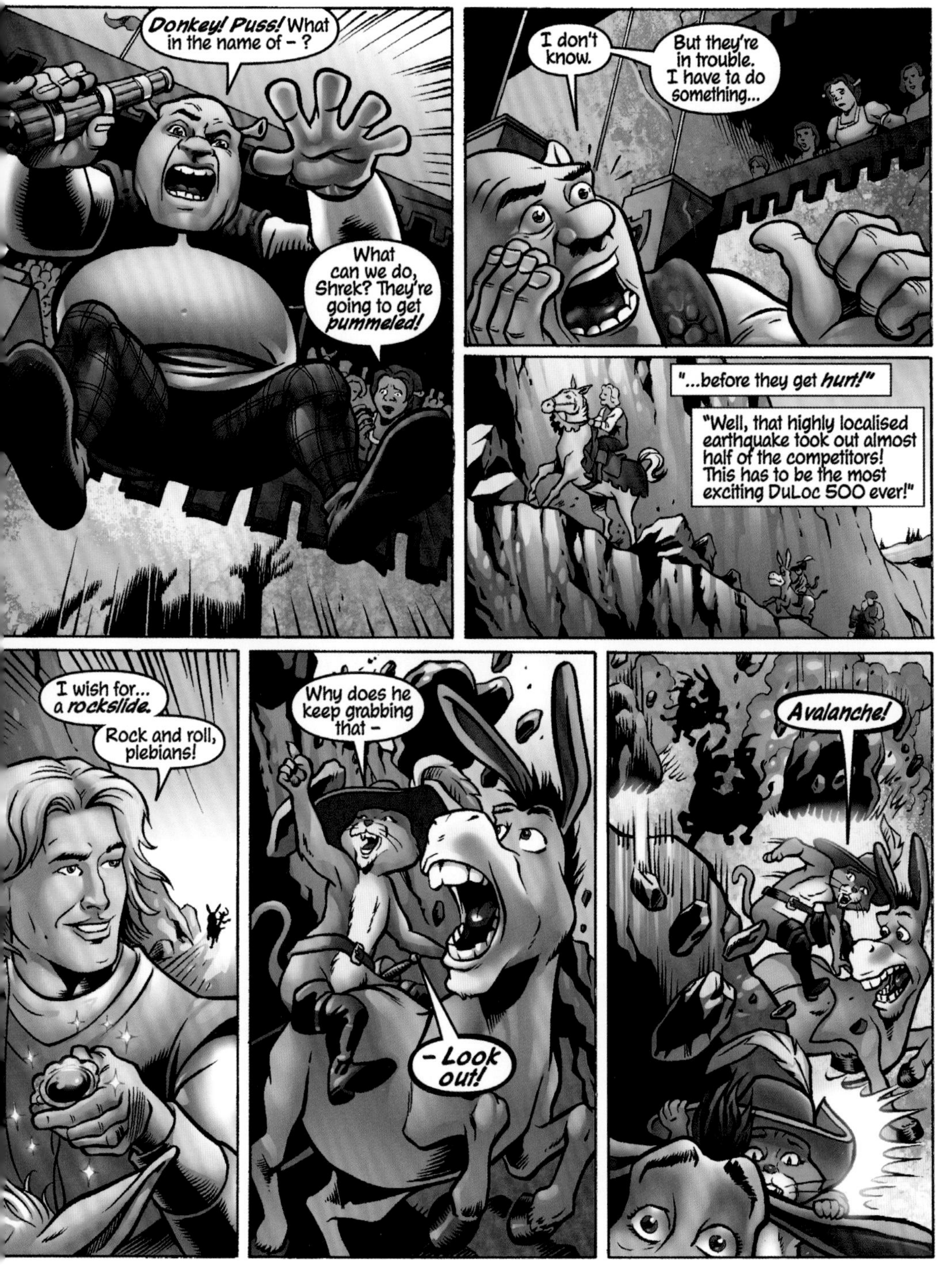

Donkey! Puss! What in the name of – ?
I don't know.
But they're in trouble. I have ta do something...
What can we do, Shrek? They're going to get pummeled!
"...before they get hurt!"
"Well, that highly localised earthquake took out almost half of the competitors! This has to be the most exciting DuLoc 500 ever!"
I wish for... a rockslide.
Rock and roll, plebians!
Why does he keep grabbing that –
– Look out!
Avalanche!

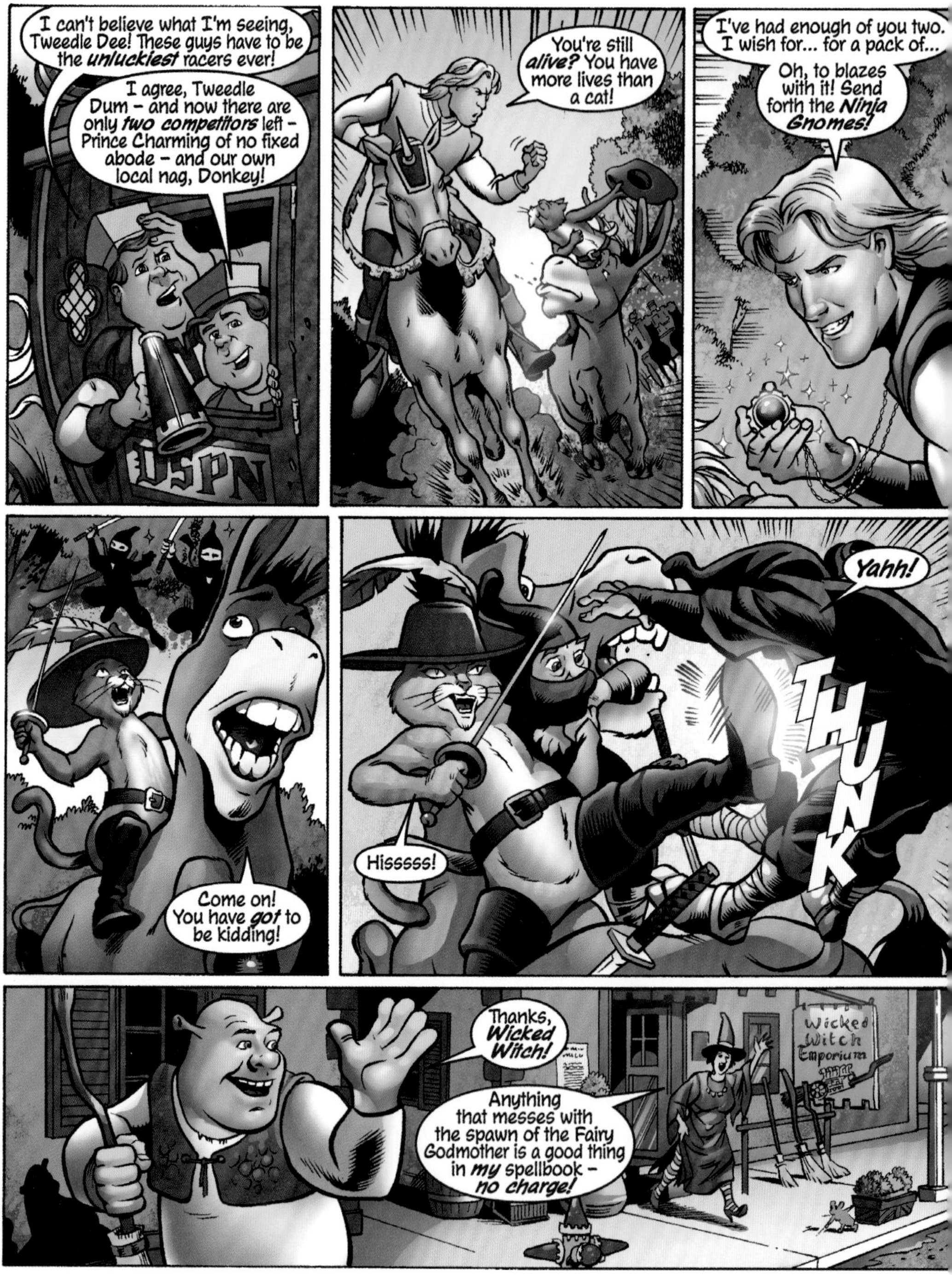
I can't believe what I'm seeing, Tweedle Dee! These guys have to be the unluckiest racers ever!
I agree, Tweedle Dum – and now there are only two competitors left – Prince Charming of no fixed abode – and our own local nag, Donkey!
DSPN
You're still alive? You have more lives than a cat!
I've had enough of you two. I wish for... for a pack of...
Oh, to blazes with it! Send forth the Ninja Gnomes!
Come on! You have got to be kidding!
Yahh!
THUNK
Hissssss!
Thanks, Wicked Witch!
Anything that messes with the spawn of the Fairy Godmother is a good thing in my spellbook – no charge!
Wicked Witch Emporium

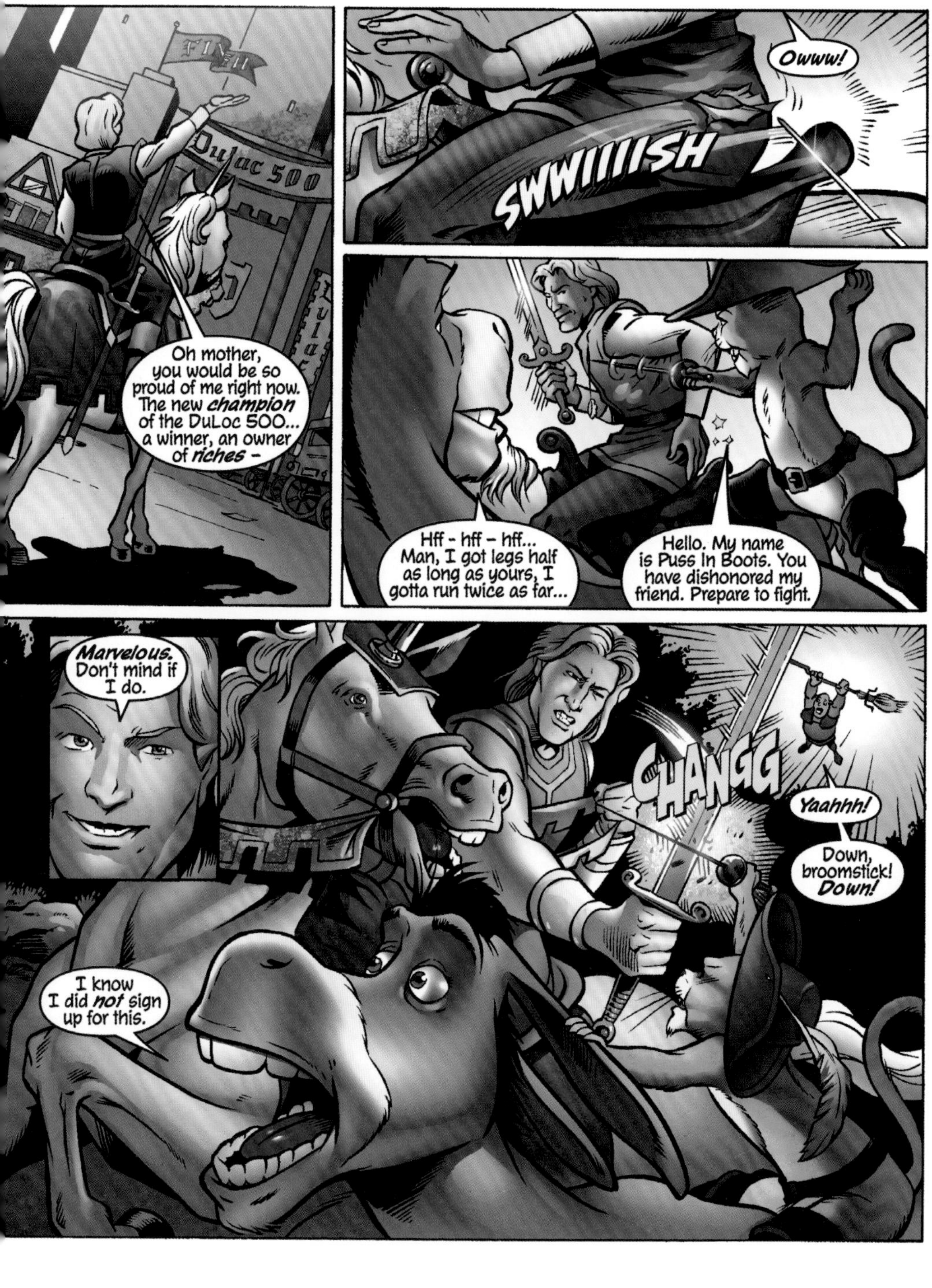
Duloc 500
Oh mother, you would be so proud of me right now. The new *champion* of the DuLoc 500... a winner, an owner of *riches* -
Owww!
SWWIIIISH
Hff - hff - hff... Man, I got legs half as long as yours, I gotta run twice as far...
Hello. My name is Puss In Boots. You have dishonored my friend. Prepare to fight.
Marvelous. Don't mind if I do.
CHANGG
Yaahhh!
Down, broomstick! *Down!*
I know I did *not* sign up for this.

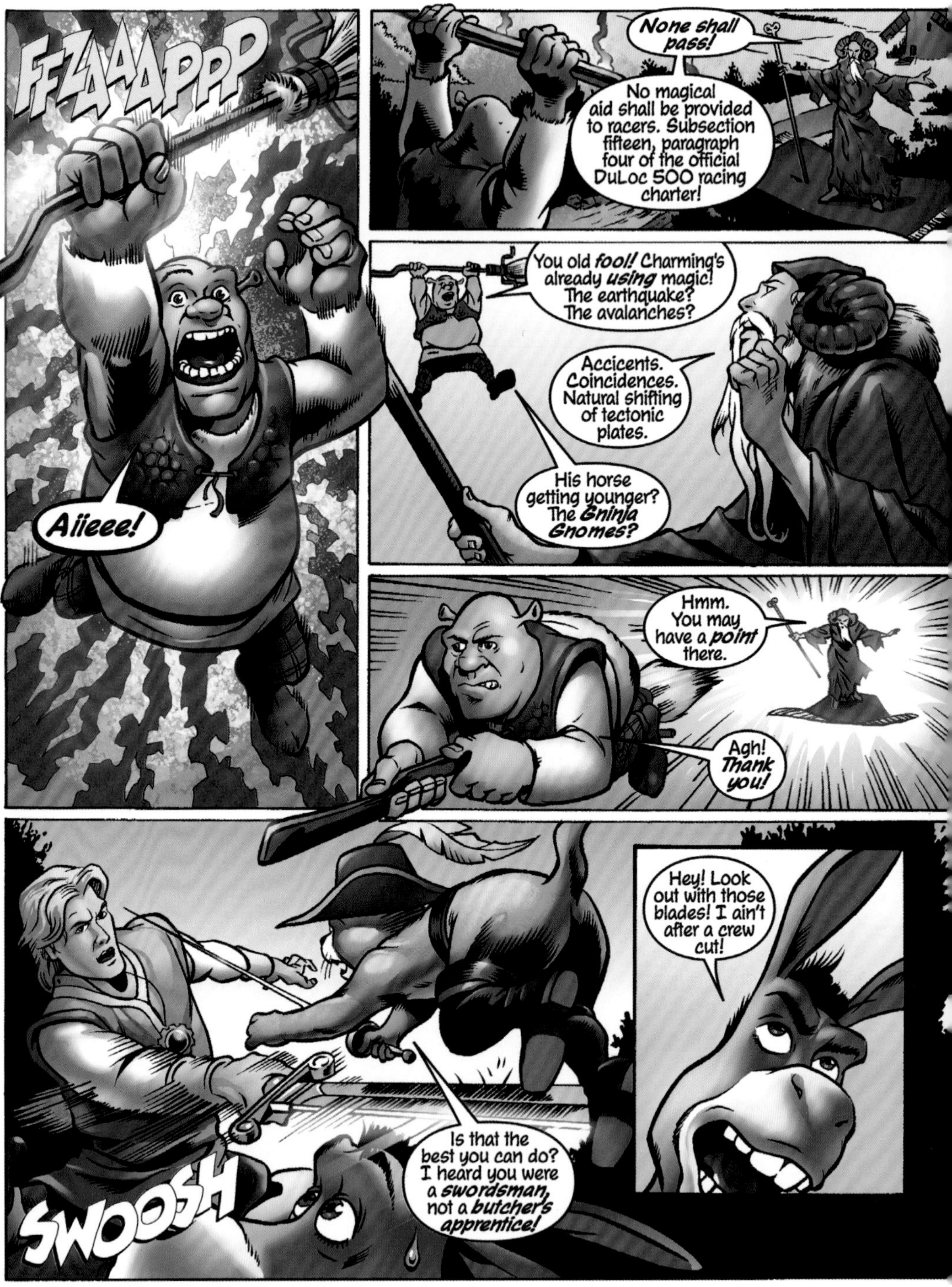
FFZAAAPPP
Aiieee!
None shall pass!
No magical aid shall be provided to racers. Subsection fifteen, paragraph four of the official DuLoc 500 racing charter!
You old *fool!* Charming's already *using* magic! The earthquake? The avalanches?
Accicents. Coincidences. Natural shifting of tectonic plates.
His horse getting younger? The *Gninja Gnomes?*
Hmm. You may have a *point* there.
Agh! *Thank you!*
Hey! Look out with those blades! I ain't after a crew cut!
Is that the best you can do? I heard you were a *swordsman,* not a *butcher's apprentice!*
SWOOSH

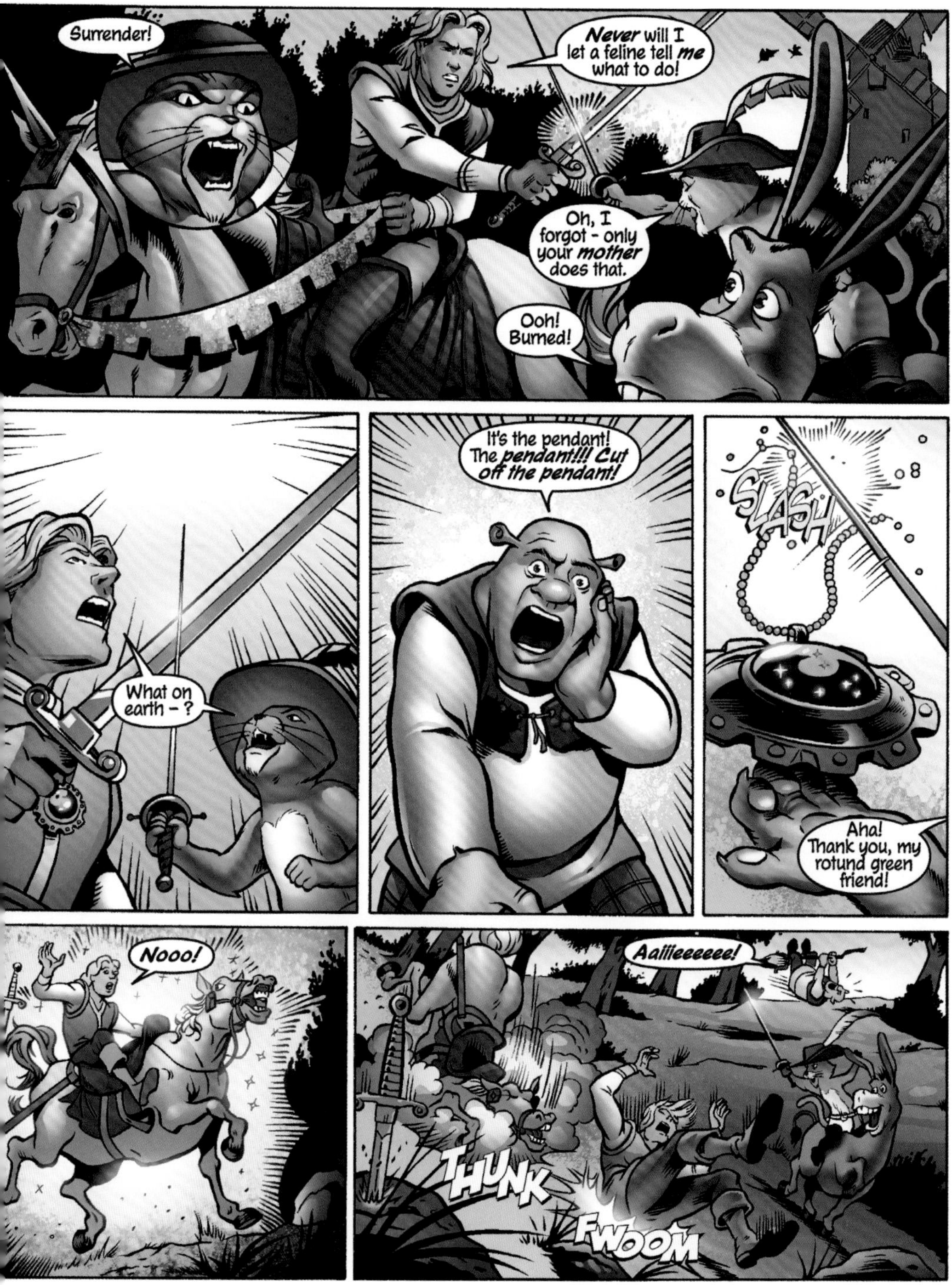
Surrender!
Never will I let a feline tell me what to do!
Oh, I forgot - only your mother does that.
Ooh! Burned!
What on earth - ?
It's the pendant! The pendant!!! Cut off the pendant!
SLASH
Aha! Thank you, my rotund green friend!
Nooo!
Aaiieeeeee!
THUNK
FWOOM

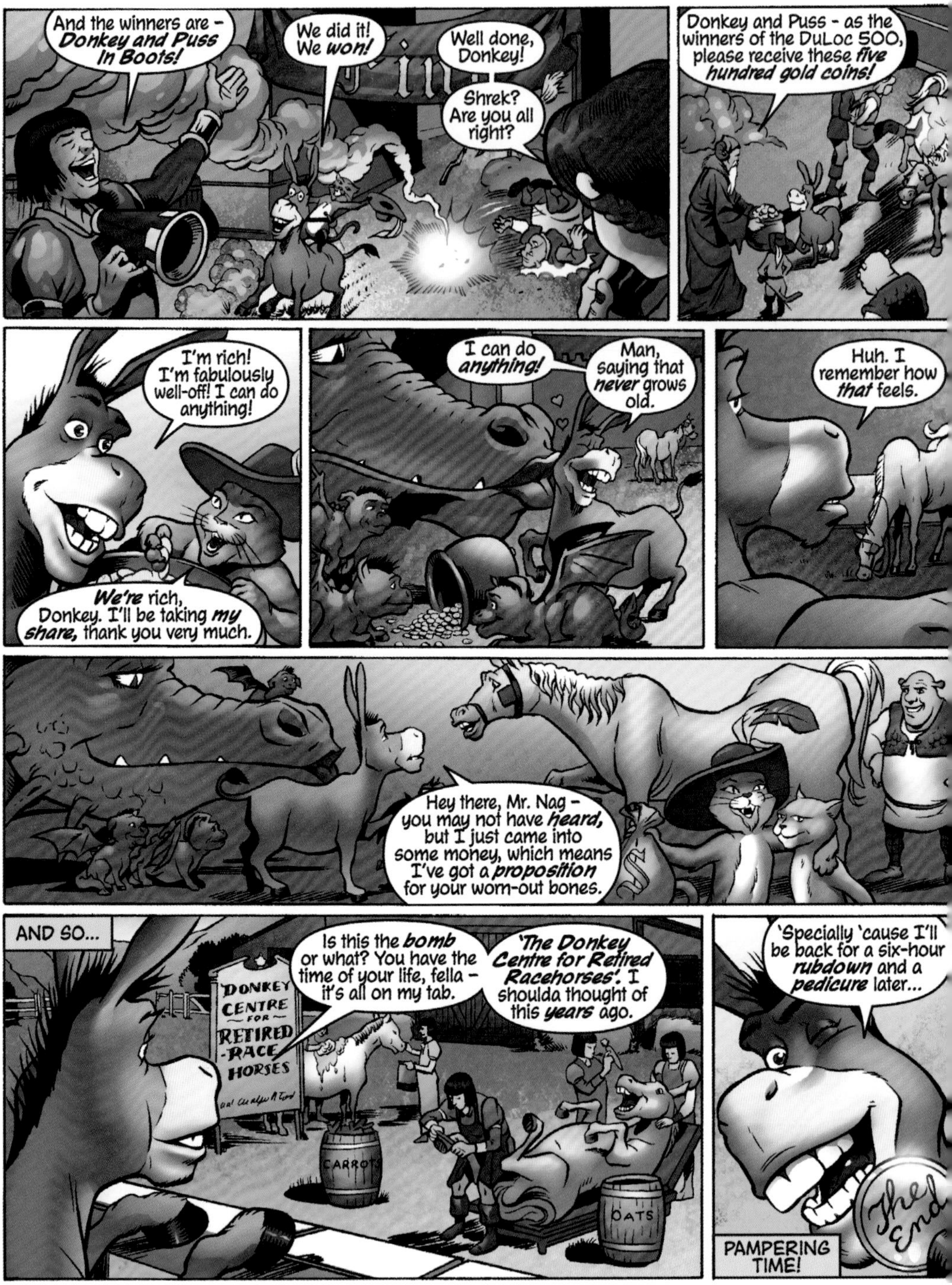
And the winners are – Donkey and Puss In Boots!
We did it! We won!
Well done, Donkey!
Shrek? Are you all right?
Donkey and Puss – as the winners of the DuLoc 500, please receive these five hundred gold coins!
I'm rich! I'm fabulously well-off! I can do anything!
We're rich, Donkey. I'll be taking my share, thank you very much.
I can do anything!
Man, saying that never grows old.
Huh. I remember how that feels.
Hey there, Mr. Nag – you may not have heard, but I just came into some money, which means I've got a proposition for your worn-out bones.
AND SO...
DONKEY CENTRE FOR RETIRED RACE HORSES
Is this the bomb or what? You have the time of your life, fella – it's all on my tab.
'The Donkey Centre for Retired Racehorses'. I shoulda thought of this years ago.
CARROTS
OATS
'Specially 'cause I'll be back for a six-hour rubdown and a pedicure later...
PAMPERING TIME!
The End

HOUSEKEEPING

WRITERS **DAN ABNETT & ANDY LANNING**
PENCILS **WES WEDMAN**
INKS **BAMBOS GEORGIOU**
COLORS **WILDIDEAS**
LETTERS **JIMMY BETANCOURT/COMICRAFT**

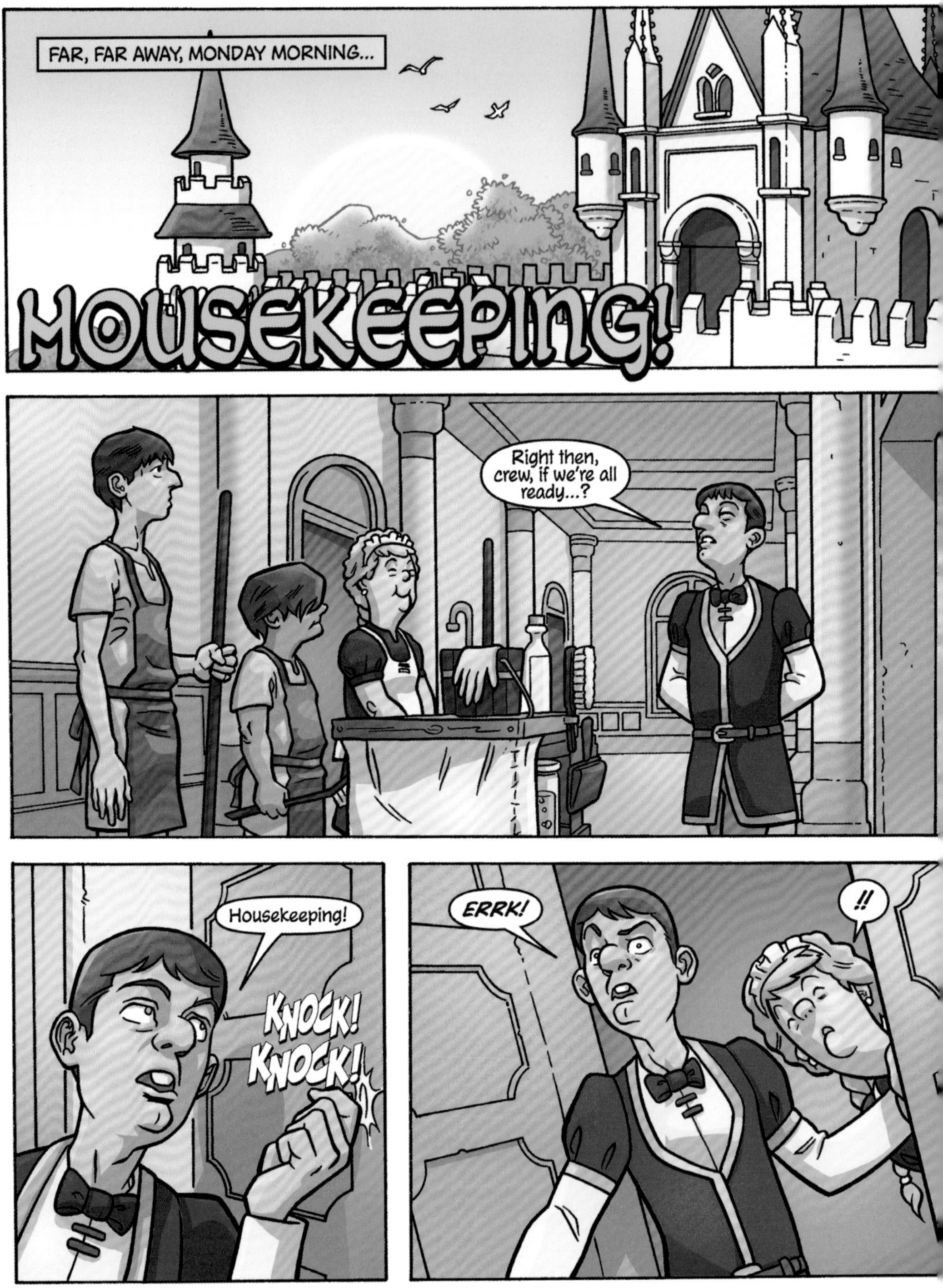
FAR, FAR AWAY, MONDAY MORNING...
HOUSEKEEPING!
Right then, crew, if we're all ready...?
Housekeeping!
KNOCK! KNOCK!
ERRK!
!!

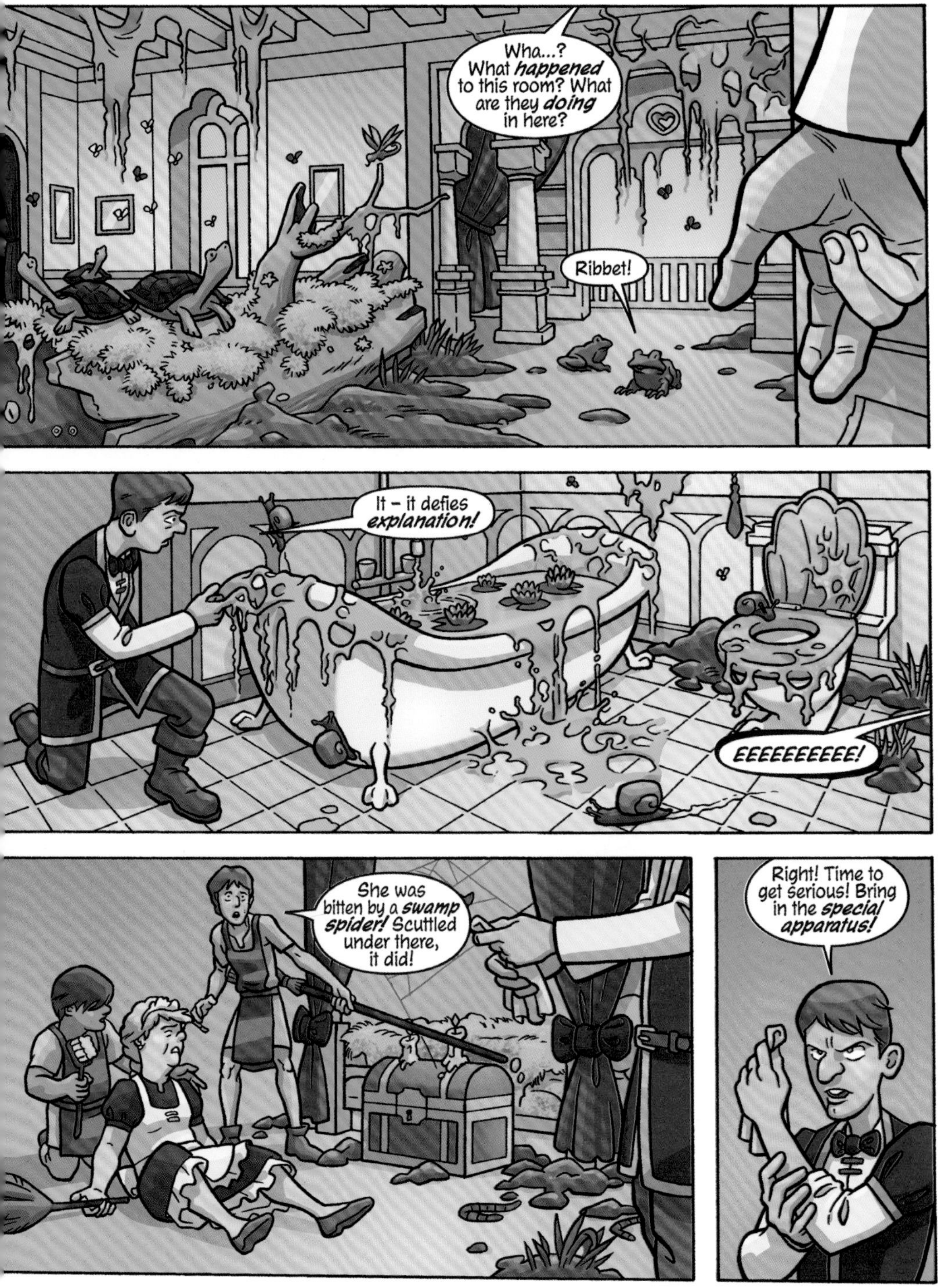
Wha...? What happened to this room? What are they doing in here?
Ribbet!
It – it defies explanation!
EEEEEEEEEE!
She was bitten by a swamp spider! Scuttled under there, it did!
Right! Time to get serious! Bring in the special apparatus!

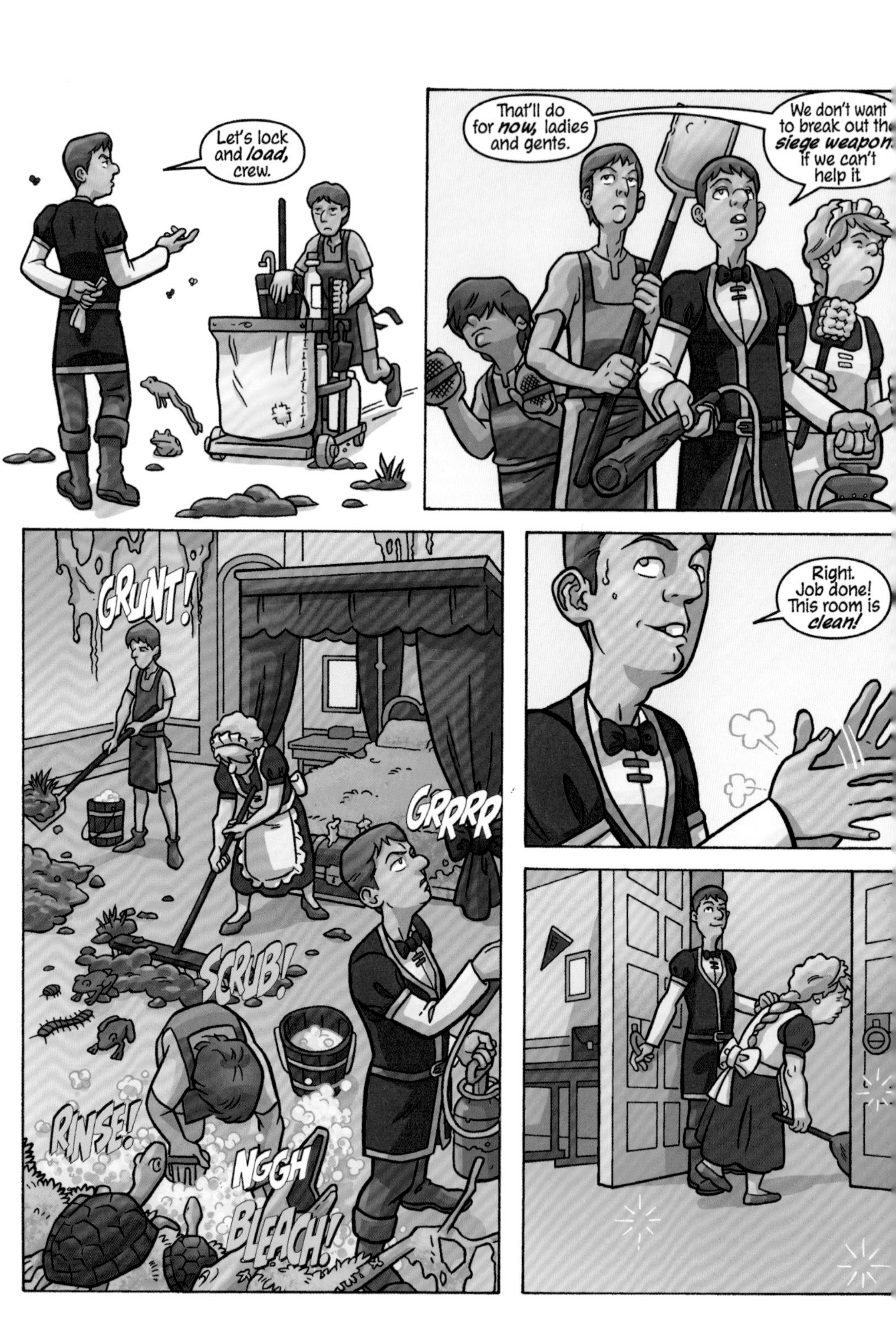
Let's lock and *load,* crew.
That'll do for *now,* ladies and gents.
We don't want to break out the *siege weapon*
if we can't help it
GRUNT!
GRRRR
SCRUB!
RINSE!
NGGH
BLEACH!
Right. Job done! This room is *clean!*

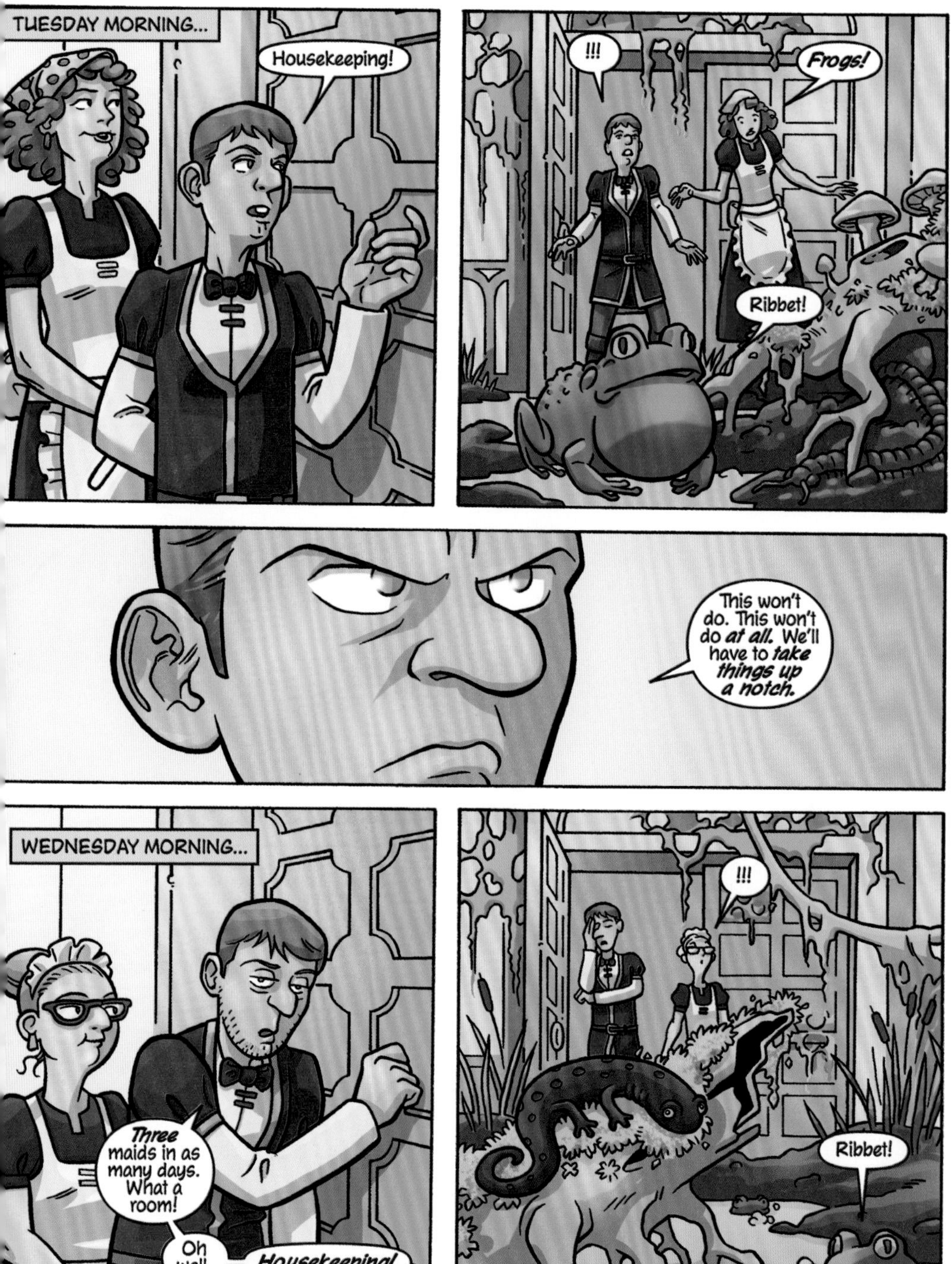

TUESDAY MORNING...
Housekeeping!
!!!
Frogs!
Ribbet!
This won't do. This won't do at all. We'll have to take things up a notch.
WEDNESDAY MORNING...
Three maids in as many days. What a room!
Oh well.
Housekeeping!
!!!
Ribbet!

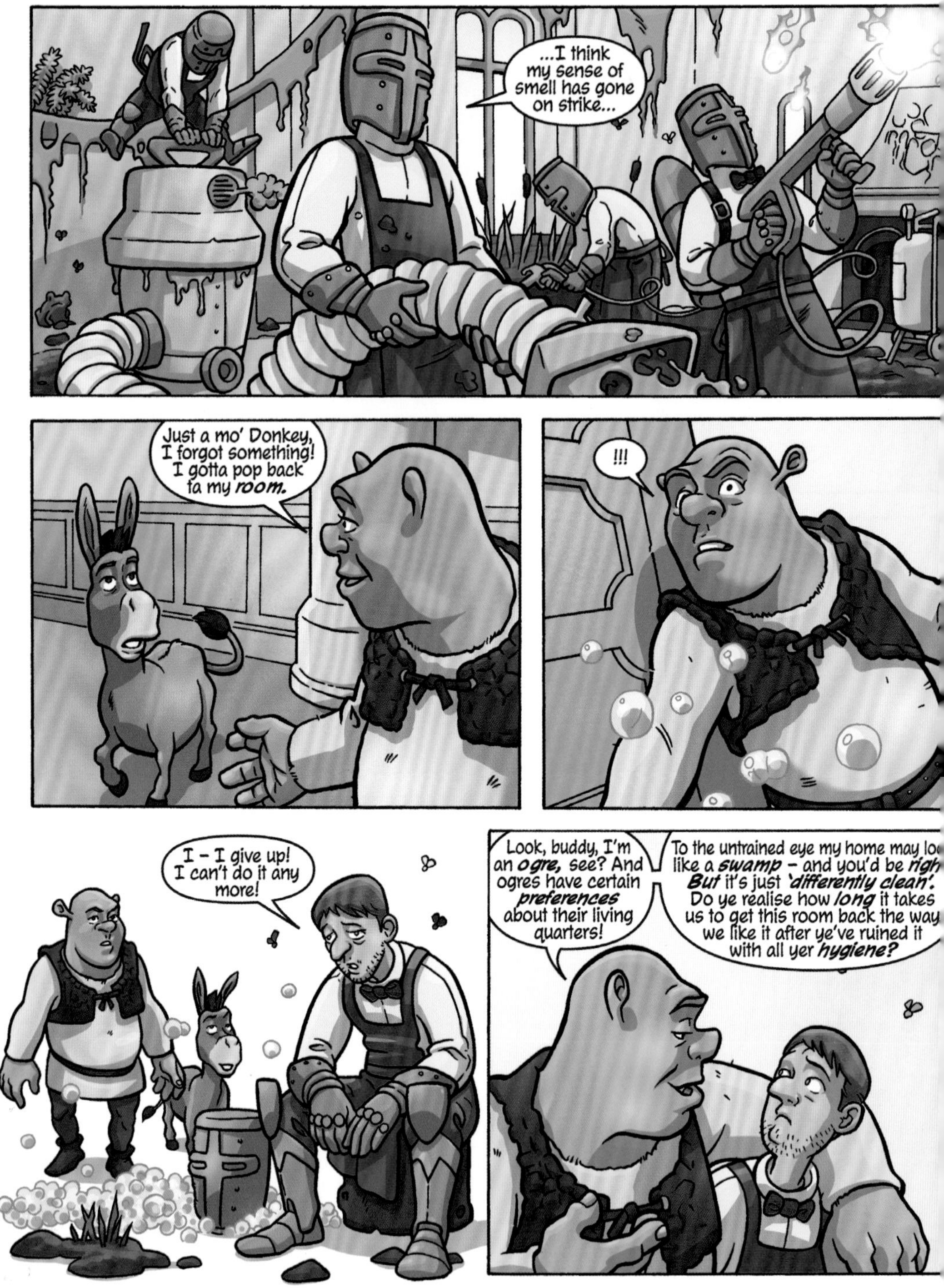
...I think my sense of smell has gone on strike...
Just a mo' Donkey, I forgot something! I gotta pop back ta my *room.*
!!!
I – I give up! I can't do it any more!
Look, buddy, I'm an *ogre,* see? And ogres have certain *preferences* about their living quarters!
To the untrained eye my home may lo like a *swamp* – and you'd be *righ* *But* it's just *'differently clean'.* Do ye realise how *long* it takes us to get this room back the way we like it after ye've ruined it with all yer *hygiene?*

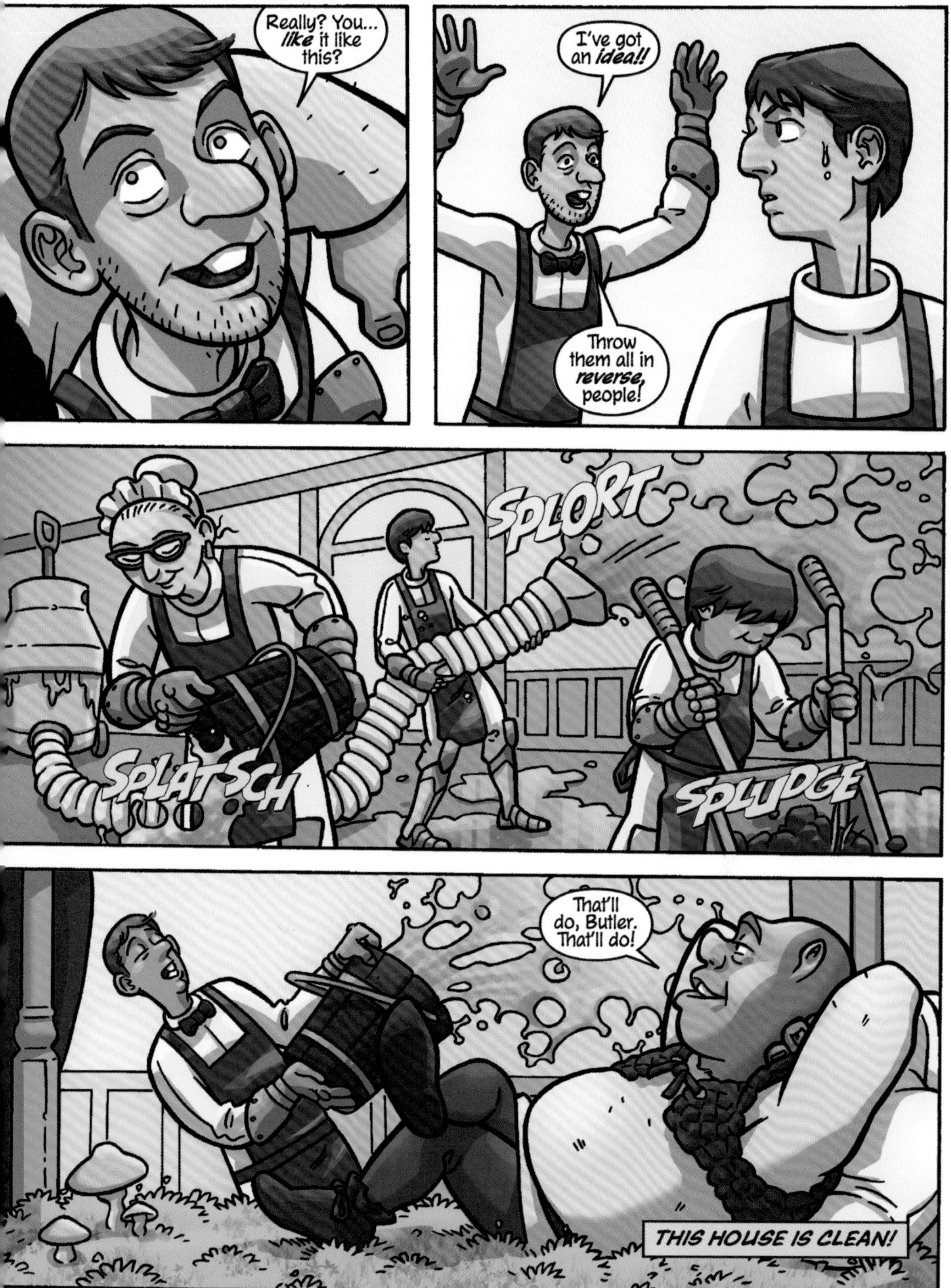
Really? You... *like* it like this?
I've got an *idea!!*
Throw them all in *reverse,* people!
SPLORT
SPLATSCH
SPLUDGE
That'll do, Butler. That'll do!
THIS HOUSE IS CLEAN!

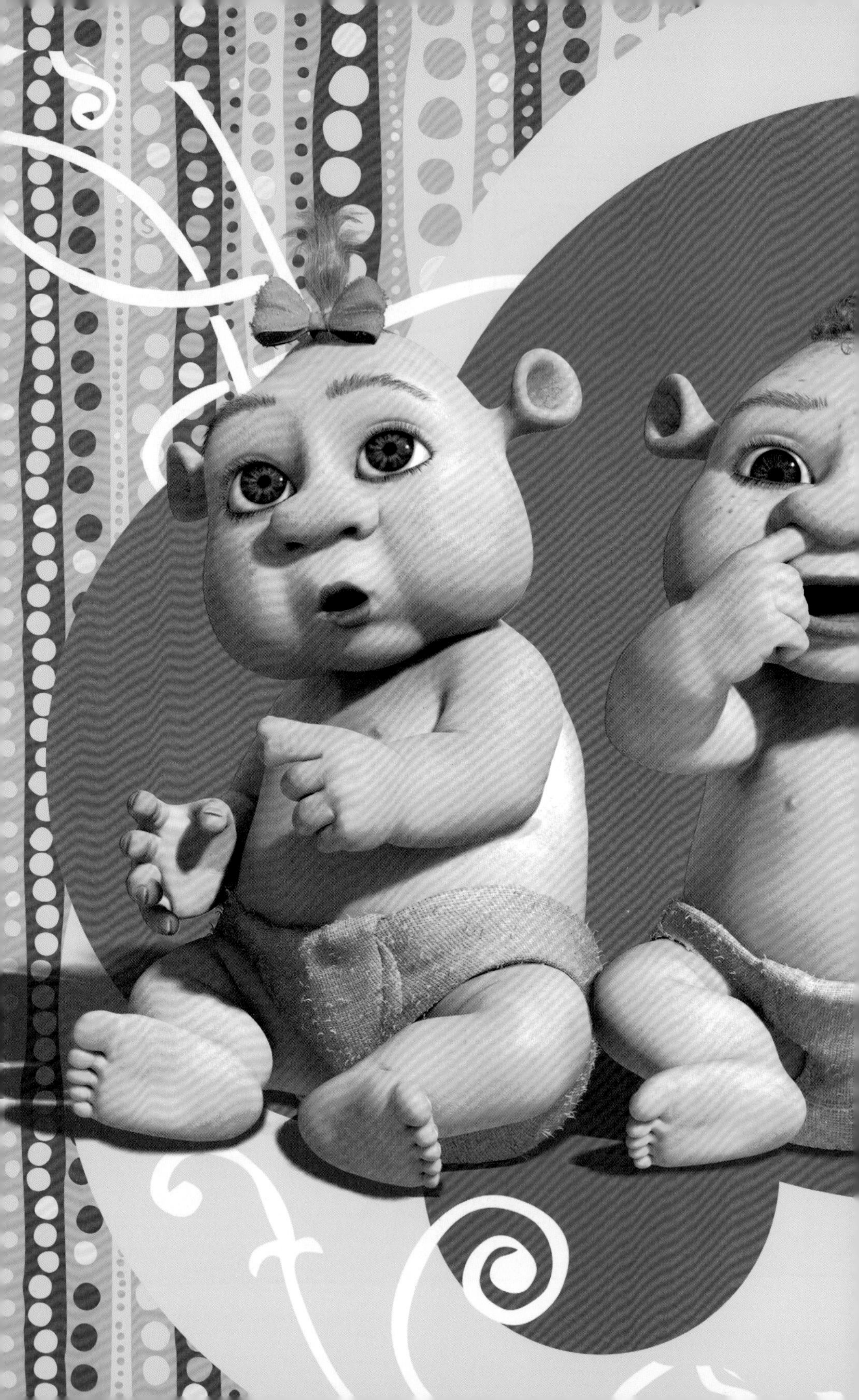

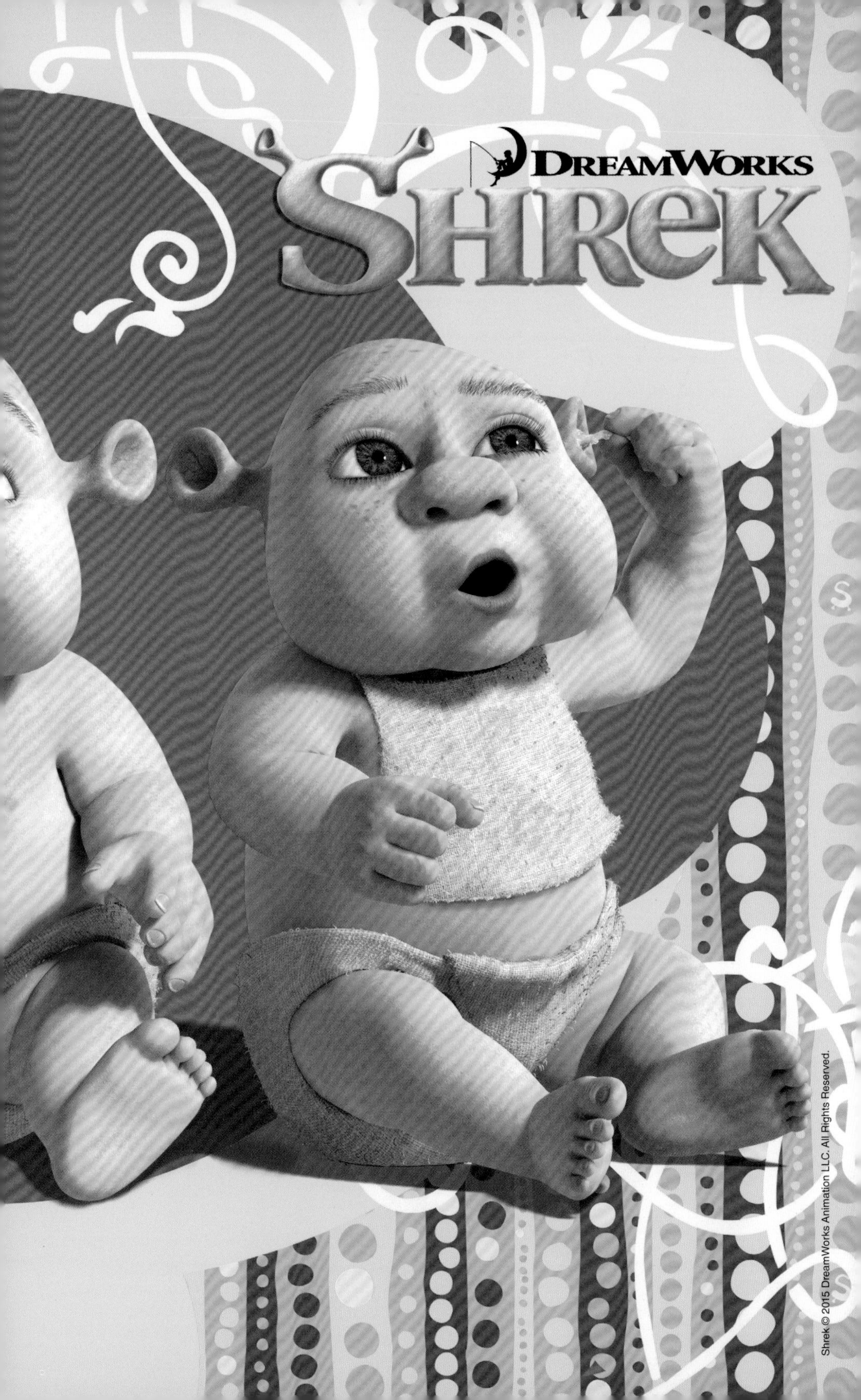
DREAMWORKS
SHREK

CONSEQUENCES

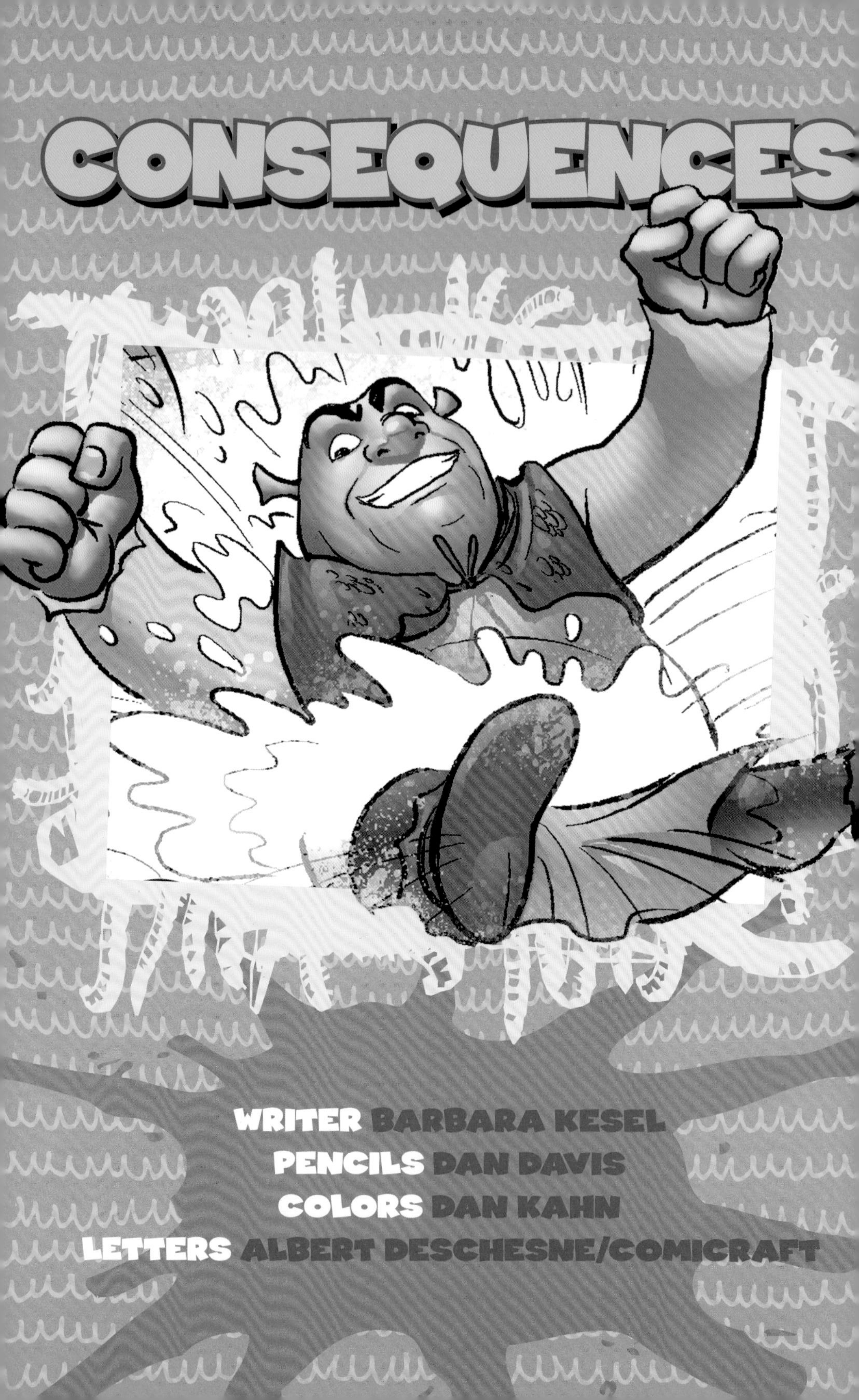

WRITER BARBARA KESEL
PENCILS DAN DAVIS
COLORS DAN KAHN
LETTERS ALBERT DESCHESNE/COMICRAFT

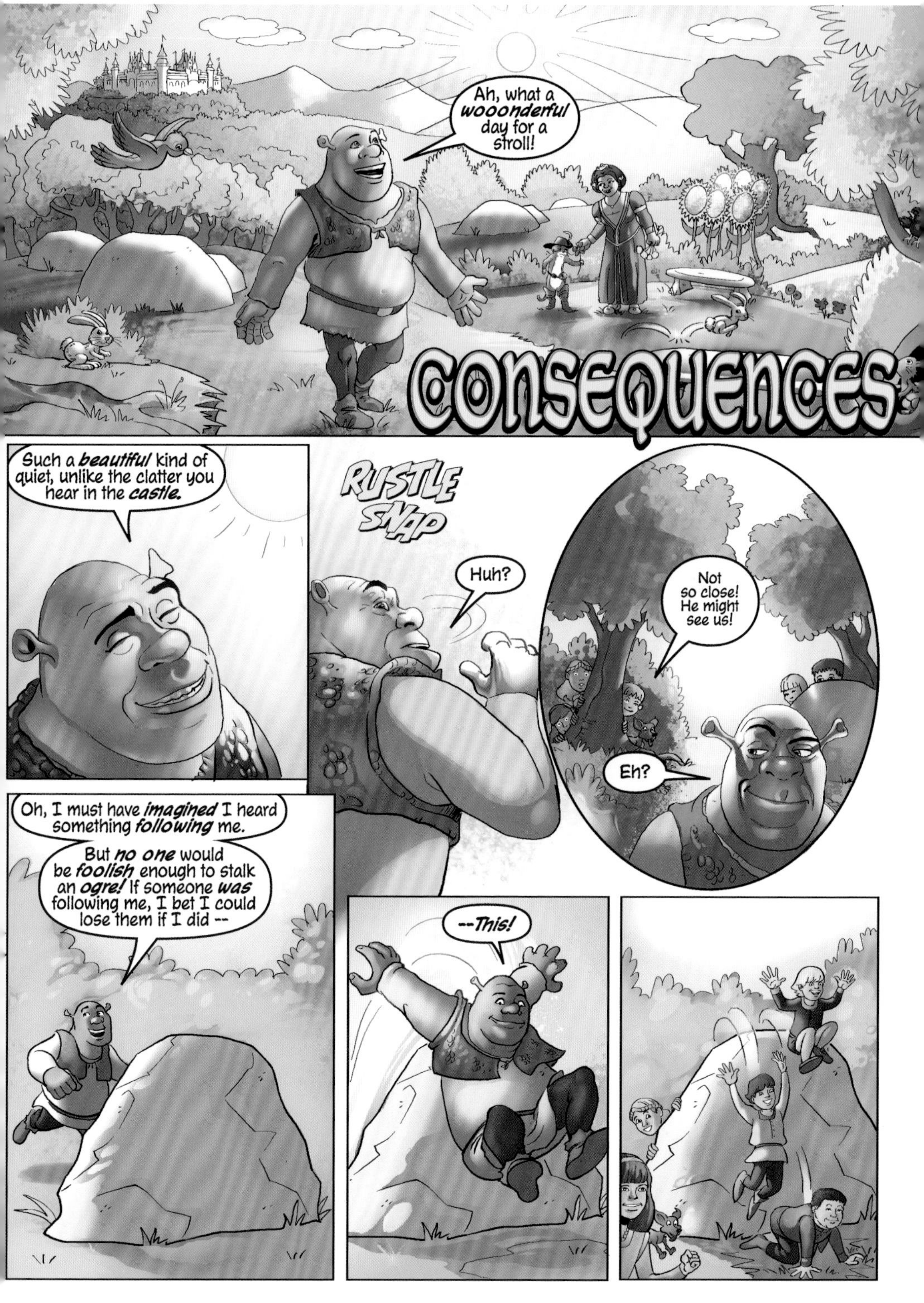
Ah, what a wooonderful day for a stroll!
CONSEQUENCES
Such a beautiful kind of quiet, unlike the clatter you hear in the castle.
RUSTLE SNAP
Huh?
Not so close! He might see us!
Eh?
Oh, I must have imagined I heard something following me.
But no one would be foolish enough to stalk an ogre! If someone was following me, I bet I could lose them if I did --
--This!

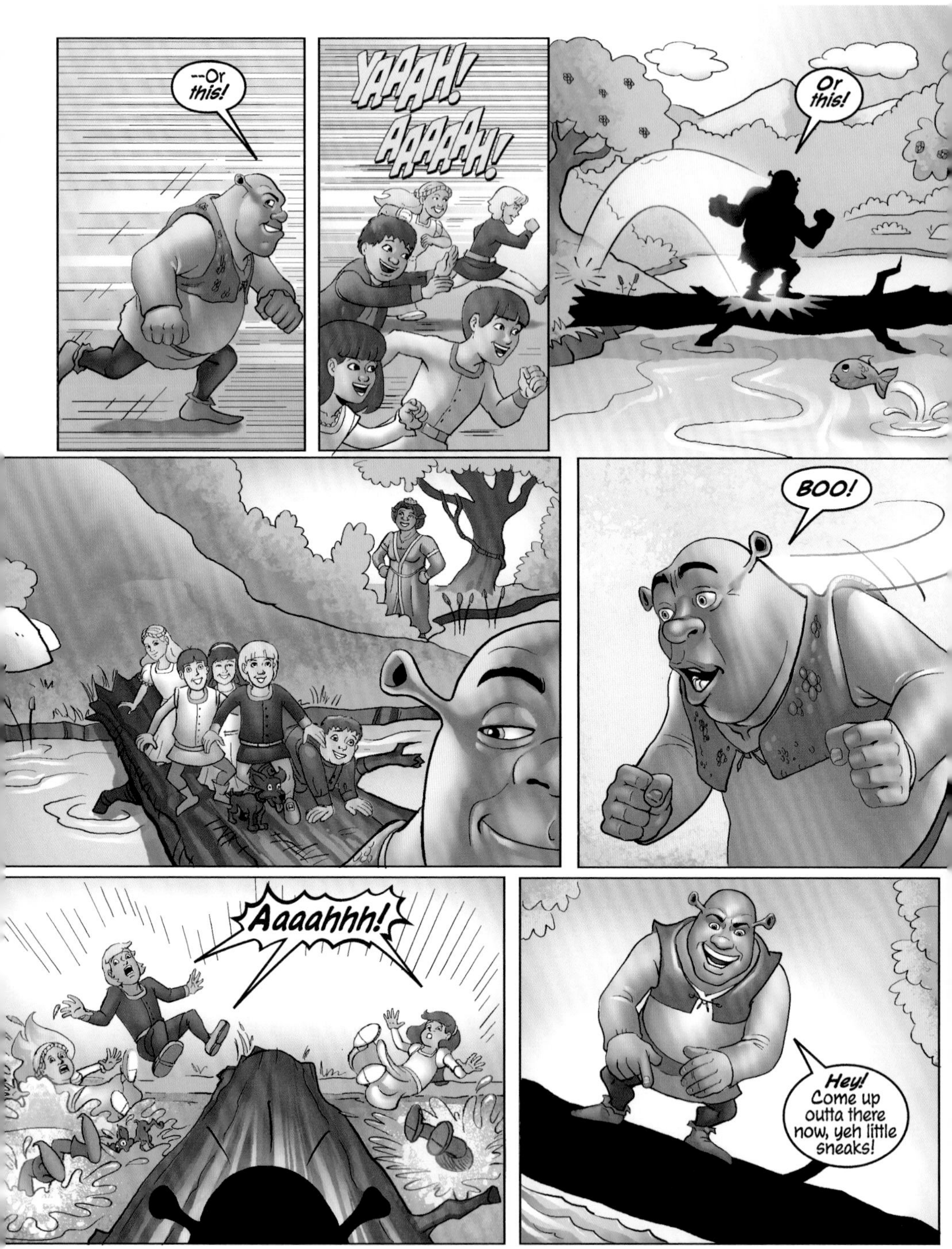
--Or this!
YAAAH!
AAAAAH!
Or this!
BOO!
Aaaahhh!
Hey! Come up outta there now, yeh little sneaks!

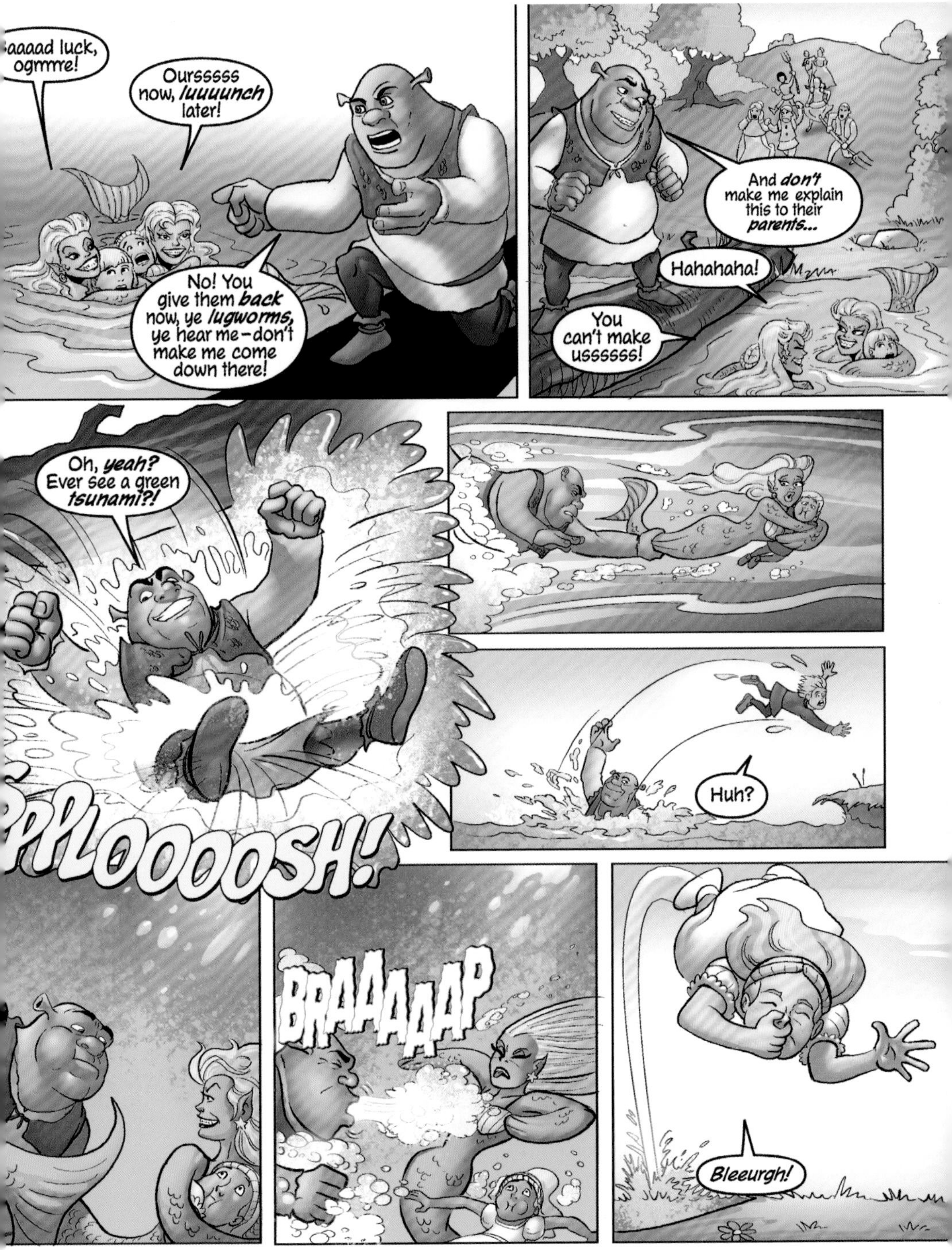

Baaaad luck, ogrrrre!
Oursssss now, luuuunch later!
No! You give them back now, ye lugworms, ye hear me–don't make me come down there!
And don't make me explain this to their parents...
Hahahaha!
You can't make ussssss!
Oh, yeah? Ever see a green tsunami?!
PPLOOOOOSH!
Huh?
BRAAAAAP
Bleeurgh!

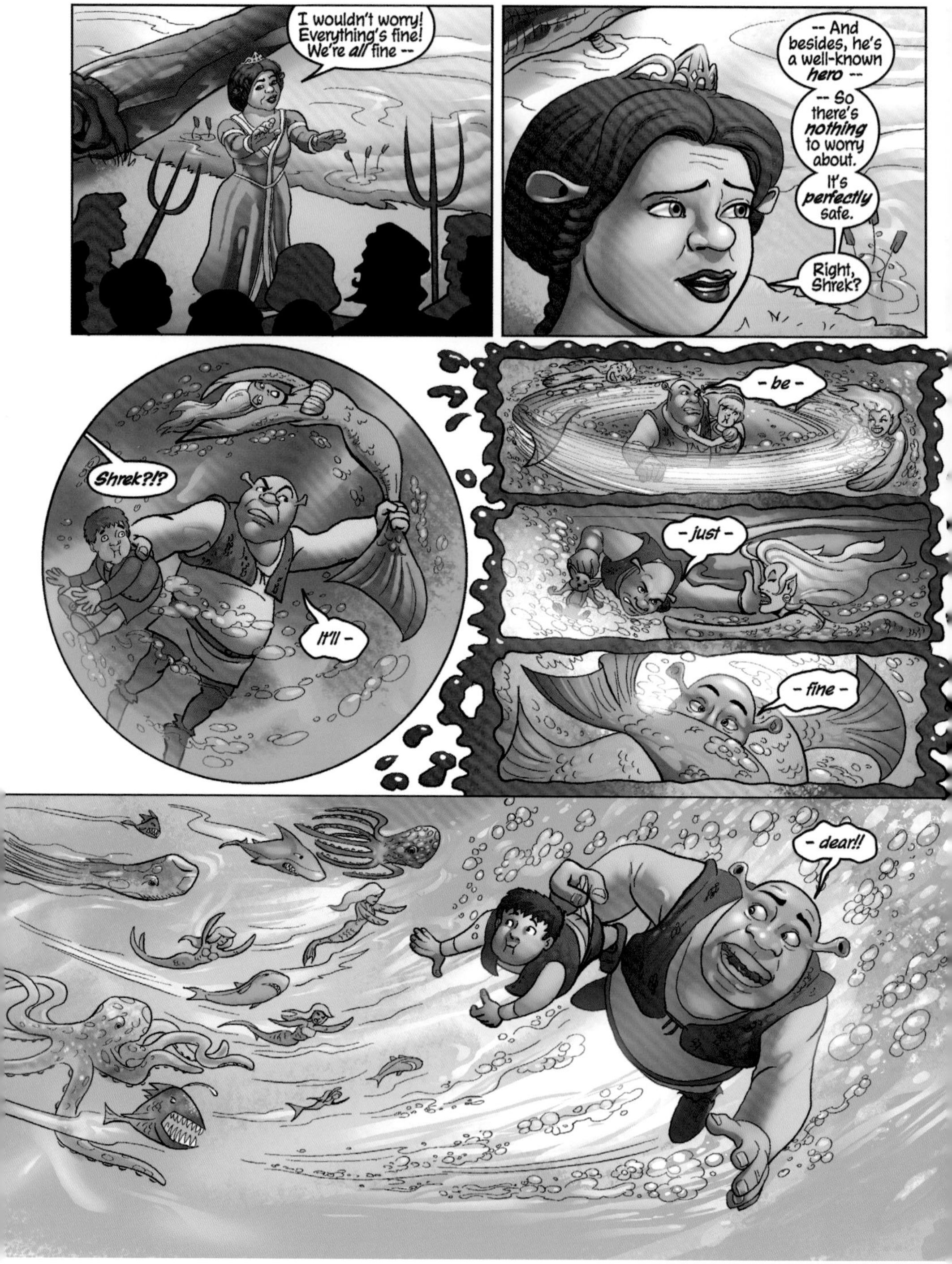
I wouldn't worry! Everything's fine! We're all fine --
-- And besides, he's a well-known hero --
-- So there's nothing to worry about.
It's perfectly safe.
Right, Shrek?
Shrek?!?
It'll -
- be -
- just -
- fine -
- dear!!

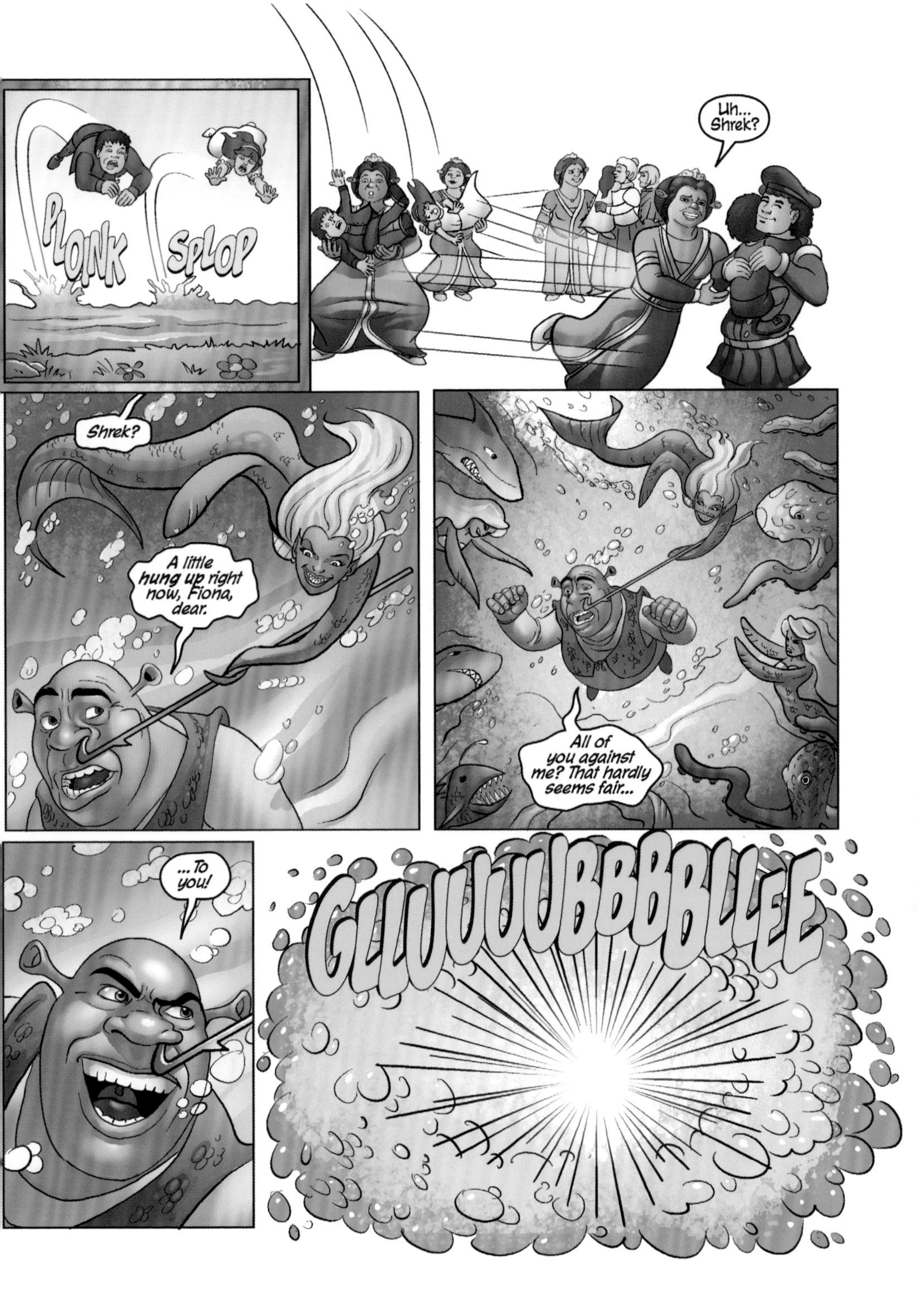
PLOINK
SPLOP
Uh... Shrek?
Shrek?
A little hung up right now, Fiona, dear.
All of you against me? That hardly seems fair...
...To you!
GLUUUUUBBBBLLEE

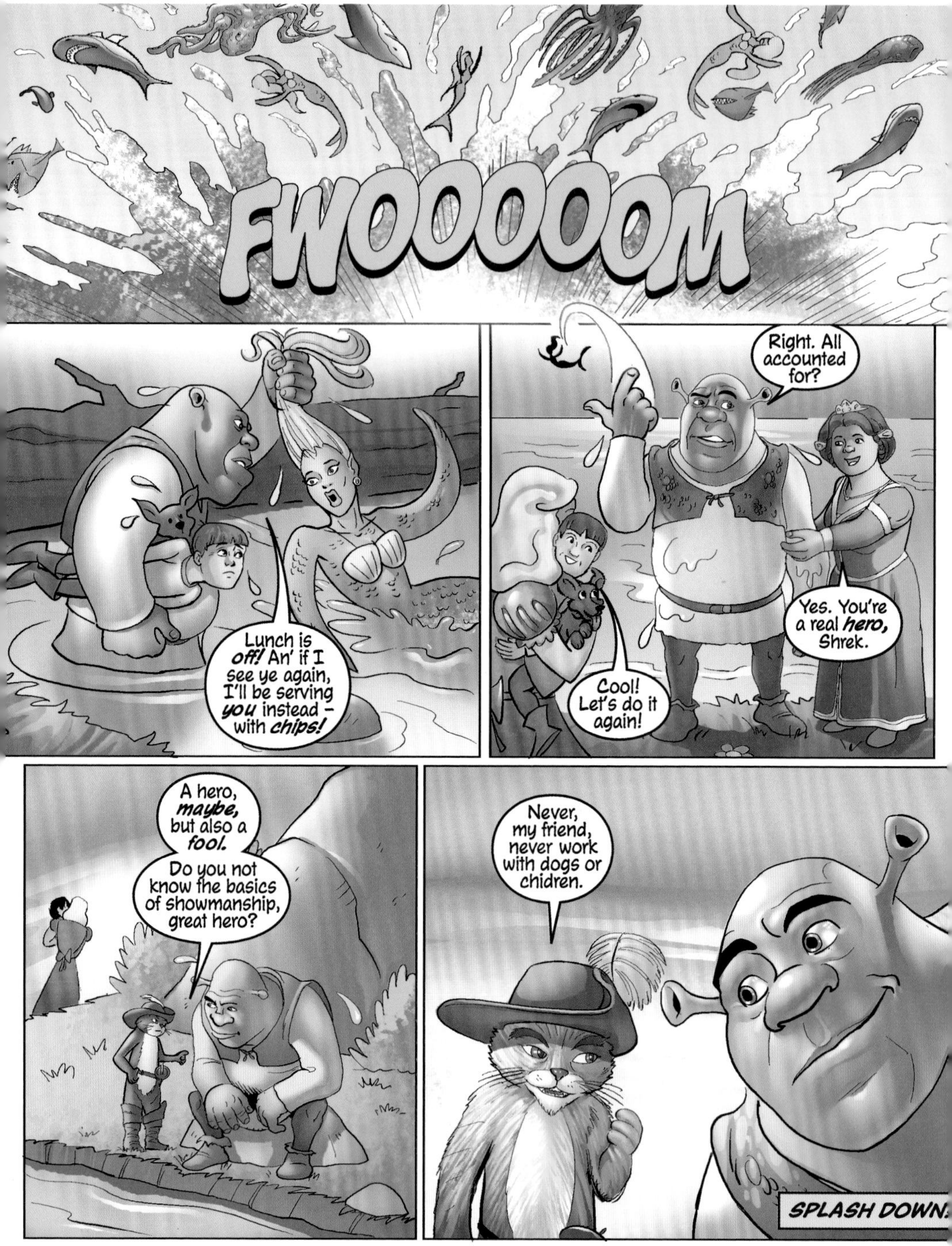
FWOOOOOM
Lunch is off! An' if I see ye again, I'll be serving you instead – with chips!
Right. All accounted for?
Cool! Let's do it again!
Yes. You're a real hero, Shrek.
A hero, maybe, but also a fool.
Do you not know the basics of showmanship, great hero?
Never, my friend, never work with dogs or chidren.
SPLASH DOWN.

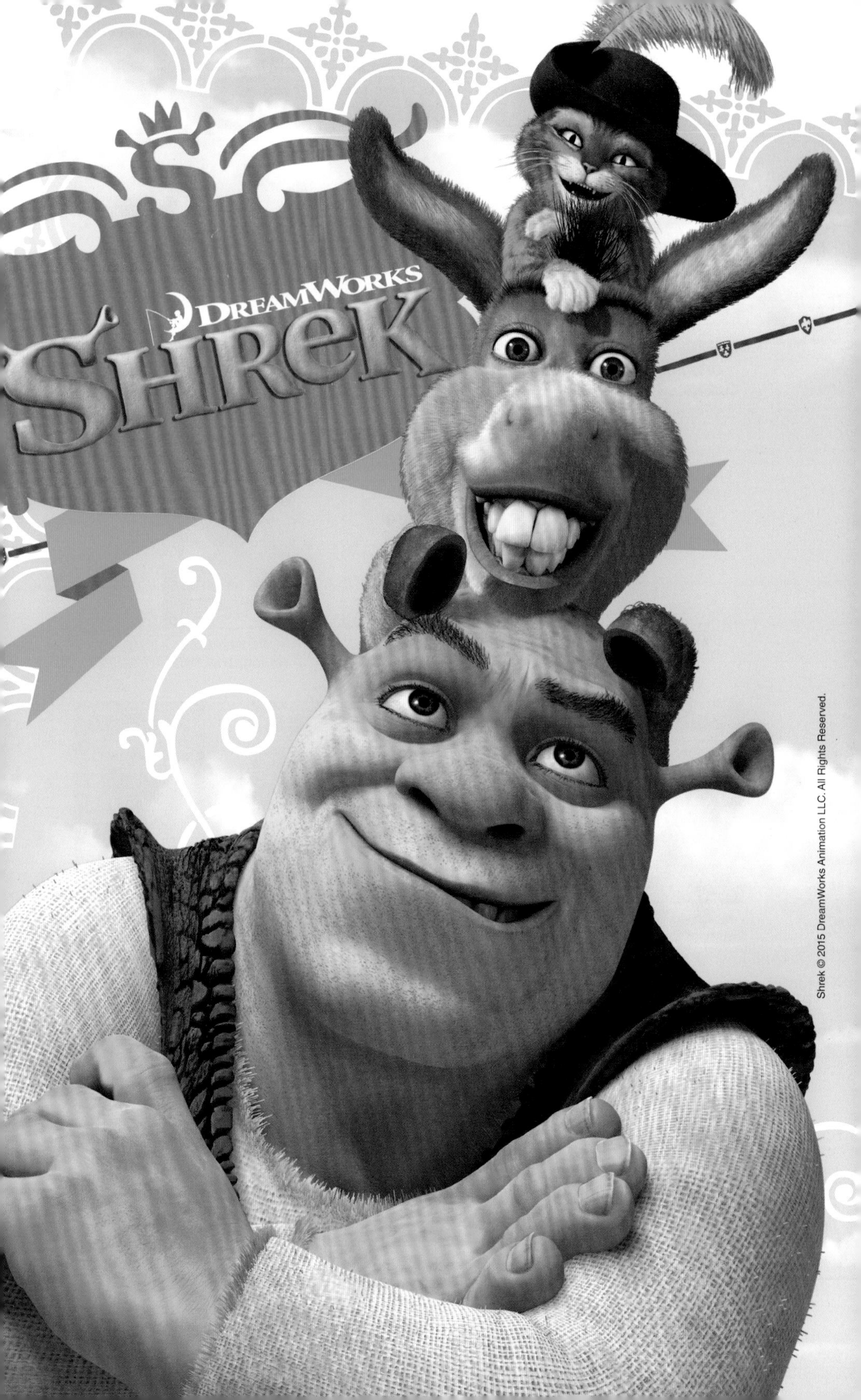
DreamWorks
Shrek

DREAMWORKS DIGESTS ALSO AVAILABLE

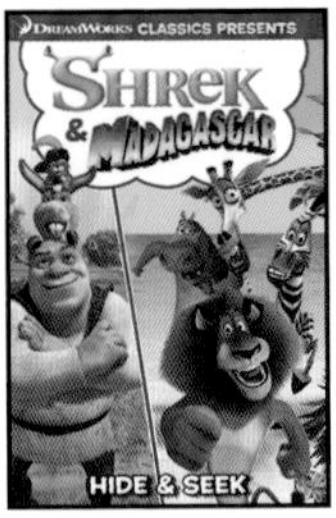
DreamWorks CLASSICS PRESENTS
SHREK & MADAGASCAR
HIDE & SEEK

Dreamworks Classics, Volume 1

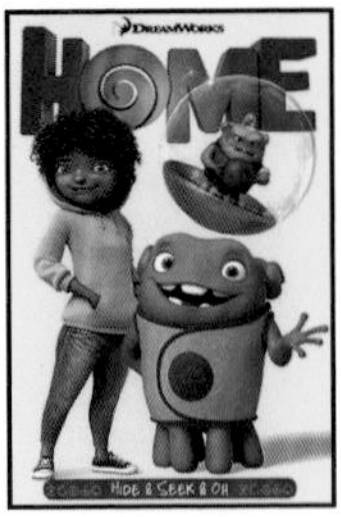
DreamWorks
HOME

Home Volume 1

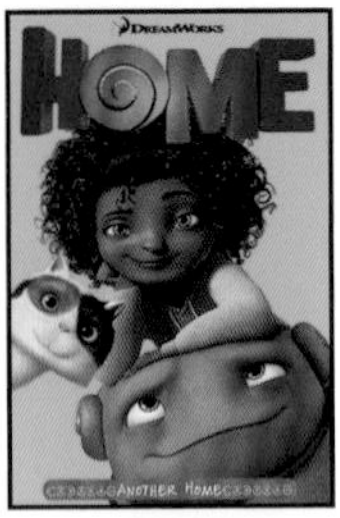
DreamWorks
HOME

Home Volume 2

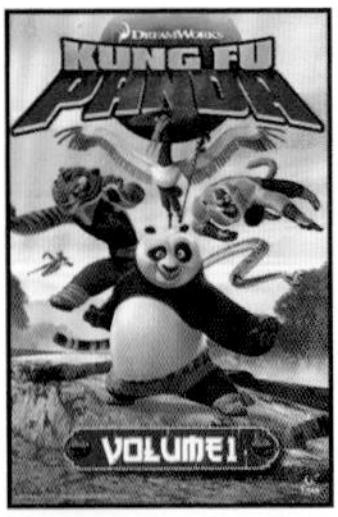
KUNG FU PANDA
VOLUME 1

Kung Fu Panda, Vol 1
Coming 12 Jan 2016

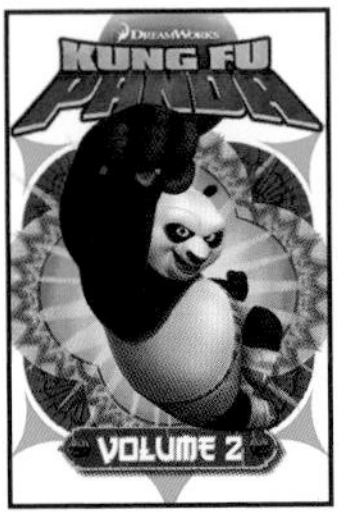
DreamWorks
KUNG FU PANDA
VOLUME 2

Kung Fu Panda, Vol 2
Coming 12 Jan 2016

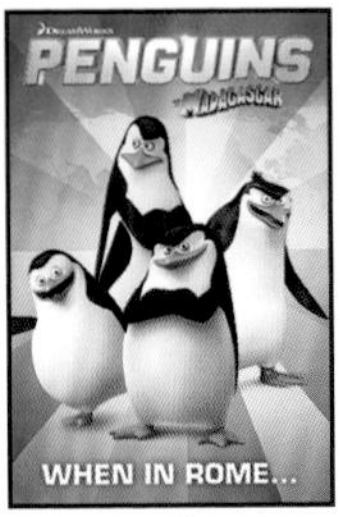
PENGUINS
WHEN IN ROME...

Penguins of Madagascar, Vol 1

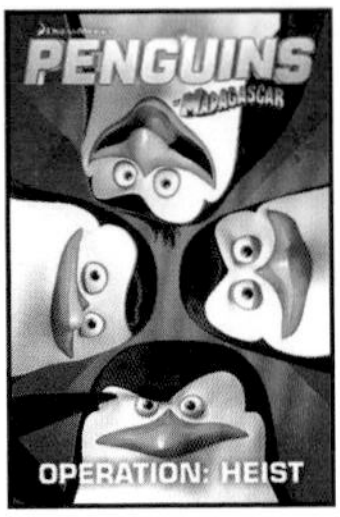
PENGUINS
OPERATION: HEIST

Penguins of Madagascar, Vol 2

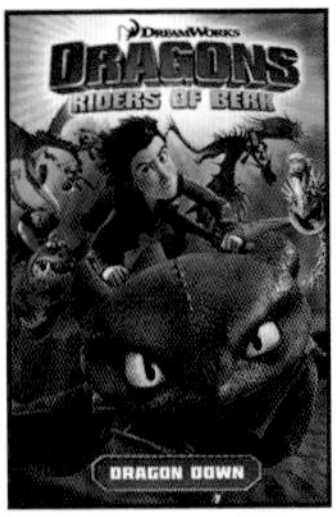
DreamWorks
DRAGONS
RIDERS OF BERK
DRAGON DOWN

DreamWorks Dragons: Riders of Berk, Vol 1

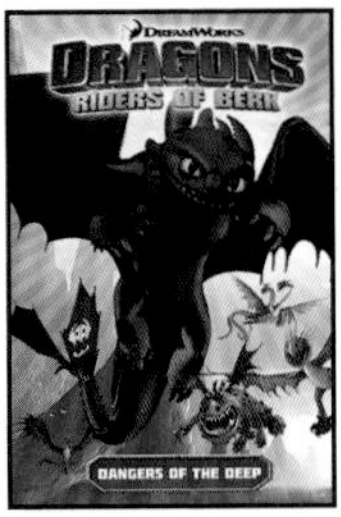
DreamWorks
DRAGONS
RIDERS OF BERK
DANGERS OF THE DEEP

DreamWorks Dragons: Riders of Berk, Vol 2

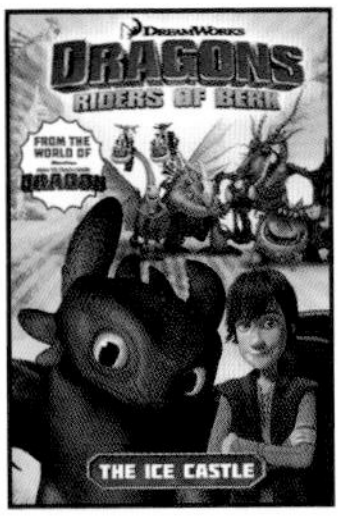
DreamWorks
DRAGONS
RIDERS OF BERK
THE ICE CASTLE

DreamWorks Dragons: Riders of Berk, Vol 3

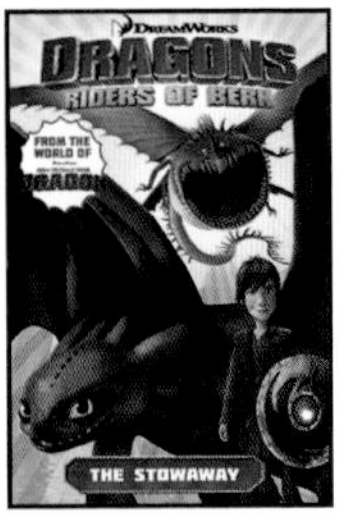
DreamWorks
DRAGONS
RIDERS OF BERK
THE STOWAWAY

DreamWorks Dragons: Riders of Berk, Vol 4

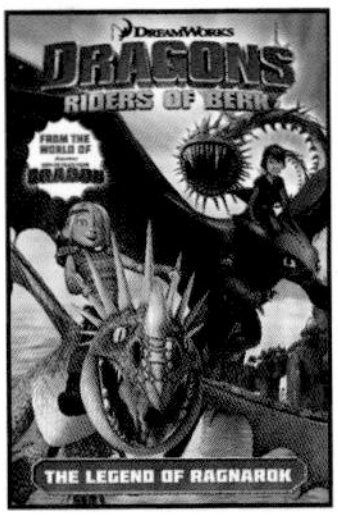
DreamWorks
DRAGONS
RIDERS OF BERK
THE LEGEND OF RAGNAROK

DreamWorks Dragons: Riders of Berk, Vol 5

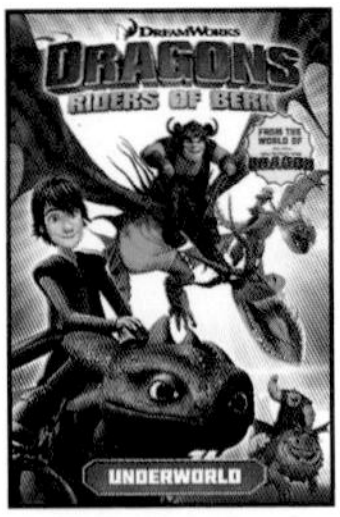
DreamWorks
DRAGONS
RIDERS OF BERK
UNDERWORLD

DreamWorks Dragons: Riders of Berk, Vol 6

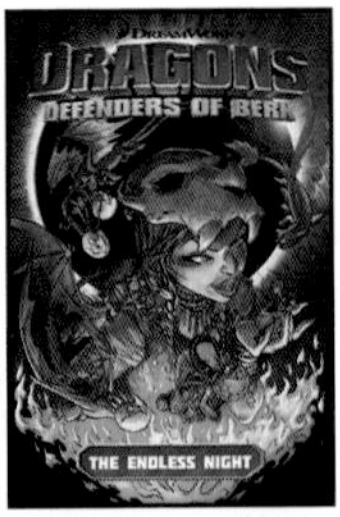
DRAGONS
DEFENDERS OF BERK
THE ENDLESS NIGHT

DreamWorks Dragons: Defenders of Berk
Coming 22 March 2016

WWW.TITAN-COMICS.COM

TITAN COMICS

DREAMWORKS ANIMATION SKG